O9-BUB-701

Thoughts, feelings…needs ran through him like quicksilver, and he was powerless to stop them, powerless to do anything other than respond to the driving need that possessed him. The driving need for him to possess her.

Katrina tried to stop what was happening, to break free of the almost bruising pressure of his kiss and pull away from him, but her lips were clinging eagerly to his, parting hotly for the hard thrust of his tongue.

Sanity, logic and her normally alert sense of self-preservation had all somehow become subservient to the thrill of longing and excitement surging through her. Under her fingertips she could feel the crispness of his thick hair, the corded muscles of his neck and the warmth of his skin. He felt so male, and so dangerous. So why wasn't she pushing him away, instead of burying her fingers in his hair and holding him closer whilst white-hot pleasure licked through her?

Arabian Nights

by
Penny Jordan

Spent at the Sheikh's pleasure…

The Sheikh's Virgin Bride #2325
One Night with the Sheikh #2332
Possessed by the Sheikh #2457

Welcome back to the exotic land of Zuran,
a beautiful romantic place
where anything is possible.

Experience a night of passion
under a desert moon
in Harlequin Presents®.

Penny Jordan

POSSESSED BY THE SHEIKH

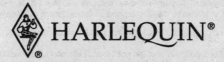

Arabian Nights

HARLEQUIN®

TORONTO • NEW YORK • LONDON
AMSTERDAM • PARIS • SYDNEY • HAMBURG
STOCKHOLM • ATHENS • TOKYO • MILAN • MADRID
PRAGUE • WARSAW • BUDAPEST • AUCKLAND

If you purchased this book without a cover you should be aware that this book is stolen property. It was reported as "unsold and destroyed" to the publisher, and neither the author nor the publisher has received any payment for this "stripped book."

ISBN 0-373-12457-0

POSSESSED BY THE SHEIKH

First North American Publication 2005.

Copyright © 2005 by Penny Jordan.

All rights reserved. Except for use in any review, the reproduction or utilization of this work in whole or in part in any form by any electronic, mechanical or other means, now known or hereafter invented, including xerography, photocopying and recording, or in any information storage or retrieval system, is forbidden without the written permission of the publisher, Harlequin Enterprises Limited, 225 Duncan Mill Road, Don Mills, Ontario, Canada M3B 3K9.

All characters in this book have no existence outside the imagination of the author and have no relation whatsoever to anyone bearing the same name or names. They are not even distantly inspired by any individual known or unknown to the author, and all incidents are pure invention.

This edition published by arrangement with Harlequin Books S.A.

® and TM are trademarks of the publisher. Trademarks indicated with ® are registered in the United States Patent and Trademark Office, the Canadian Trade Marks Office and in other countries.

www.eHarlequin.com

Printed in U.S.A.

CHAPTER ONE

KATRINA was standing in the middle of the souk when she saw him. She had been about to start bargaining with the stallholder for a length of embroidered silk she had picked up, when something made her turn her head. He was standing on the other side of the narrow alleyway dressed in a traditional white *disha-dasha*, the sunlight filtering striking shards of light against the honey-coloured warmth of his skin, and glittering on the cruelly sharp-looking knife that was thrust into his belt.

Sensing that he had lost her attention, the stallholder looked past her, following the direction of her helplessly enmeshed gaze.

'He is from the Ayghar Tuareg Tribe,' he said.

Katrina made no response. She knew from the research she had done before coming out to Zuran that the Ayghar Tuaregs had been a fierce tribe of warriors who, in previous centuries, had been paid to escort the trading caravans across the desert, and the tribe still preferred their traditional nomadic way of life.

Unlike other robed men she had seen, he was cleanshaven. His eyes, glittering over her with a haughty lack of interest, were heart-stoppingly dark amber, set with flecks of pure gold between the thickness of his black lashes.

They, like him, reminded her of the magnificence of a dangerous predator; something, someone who could never be tamed or constrained in the cage of modern urban civilisation. This was a man of the desert, a man who made and then lived by a moral code of his own devising. There was an arrogance about his features and his stance that both appalled her and yet at the same time compelled her to keep looking at him.

And he had a dangerously passionate mouth!

An unwanted sensual shiver skittered along her spine as she was caught off guard by the unexpected detour of her own thoughts.

She was not here in the desert kingdom of Zuran to think about men with dangerously passionate mouths. She was here as part of a visiting team of dedicated scientists working to protect the area's natural flora and fauna, she reminded herself firmly. But still she couldn't stop watching him.

Seemingly oblivious of her, he glanced up and down the alleyway of the busy bazaar. It truly was a scene from an Arabian fantasy come to life, at least so far as Katrina was concerned, although she knew that her boss, Richard Walker, would have derided her contemptuously if she were ever to say so in his presence. But she didn't want to think about Richard. Despite the fact that she had made it plain to him that she wasn't interested in him, and in addition to the fact that he was a married man, Richard had been subjecting her to a toxic mix of unpleasant sexual interest combined with outright nastiness when she rejected his advances.

Just thinking about Richard and his unwanted pursuit of her was enough to make her shrink back into the shadows of the stall. Immediately the amber gaze found and trapped her, pillaging the shadows for her, and making her shrink instinctively even further into them without seeking to analyse why she should feel the need to do such a thing.

But even though the shadows were surely concealing her, she could see that he had focused on exactly where she was. Her heart drummed a warning tattoo, and she could feel an anxious beading of perspiration break out on her skin.

A group of black-robed and veiled women walking down the alleyway came between them, cutting off her view of him and, she hoped, his view of her. By the time they had gone and she could see him again it was obvious that he had lost interest in her because he was turning away, pulling the loose end of the indigo-dyed cloth wrapped around his head over his face as he did so, so that only his eyes could be seen, in the traditional manner of men of the Tuareg tribe. Then, with his back to her, he turned to enter the doorway behind him, his height forcing him to duck his head.

Katrina noticed that the hand he had placed on the door frame was lean and brown, long-fingered, his nails well cared for. A small frown pleated her forehead. She knew a great deal about the nomad tribes of the Arabian desert and their history and it struck her sharply how much of an anomaly it was, both that a supposed Tuareg tribesman should go against centuries of tradition and reveal his face for the world to see, and additionally that a member of a tribe so well known for their indigo-dyed clothes that they were often referred to as 'blue men' should have such manicured hands that would not disgrace a millionaire businessman.

Her stomach muscles tensed and her heart lurched against her ribs. She was no foolish, impressionable girl ready to believe that every man in a *disha-dasha* was a powerful leader of men, and nor was she hiding some secret fantasy desire for sex in the sand with such a man! She was a qualified scientist of twenty-four! And yet…

As he finally disappeared through the doorway she let out her pent-up breath in a leaky sigh of relief.

'You want this? It's very fine silk… Very fine. And a very good price.'

Obediently she gave her attention to the silk. It was gossamer-fine and just the right shade of ice-blue for her own strawberry-blonde colouring. Because she was out in public on her own, she had taken the pre-caution of scraping her hair back off her face and tucking it up into the deep brimmed hat she was wearing.

But in such a fabric her body could be tantalisingly semi-revealed by its gauzy layers, and she could let her hair down in a silken cloud as a man with golden lion eyes looked upon her…

Katrina let the silk drop from her fingers as though it had burned her. As the stallholder picked it up a group of uniformed men came striding into the alley, causing people to scatter as they pushed past them, thrusting open doors and pulling coverings from stalls, quite plainly looking for someone and equally plainly not caring what damage they might cause to either people or belongings as they did so.

For some reason she could not understand, Katrina's gaze went to the door through which the tribesman had disappeared.

The uniformed men were on a level with her now.

Behind her the door opened and a man stepped into the street. Tall and dark-haired, he was wearing

European clothes—chinos and a linen shirt—but Katrina recognised him immediately, her eyes widening in surprise.

The tribesman had become a European. He turned and started to walk down the alleyway. He had just drawn level with the stall where Katrina was standing when one of the uniformed men saw him and pushed past Katrina, calling out to him in English and Zuranese.

'You! Stop!'

Katrina saw the way the tribesman's golden gaze hardened, checking, searching...and then stopping as it alighted on her.

'Darling! There you are—I warned you not to go wandering off without me.'

The lean fingers she had noticed only minutes ago were now manacling her wrist, sliding down over her hand and entwining with her own, in a parody of a lover's intimacy, holding her hand fast in a locked grip she couldn't break. A smile that was merely a calculated curling of his mouth briefly broke up the hard arrogance of his face. He took a step towards her.

'I am not your darling,' Katrina told him breathlessly.

'Start walking...' he told her quietly, the intimidating, hard gaze imprisoning her under its magnetic spell.

Hostility darkened the normal gentleness of her own speedwell-blue eyes, but it was a hostility that was spiked with something much more primitive and dangerous, she admitted numbly as she did as he was instructing her. He moved closer to her and through the hot, sun-baked scent of spices and perfumes she was sharply aware of, first, the discreet expensive lemony scent of his cologne, and then far more disturbingly as he moved closer to her the intimate, faintly musky scent of his body itself.

The alleyway was full of armed men now, pushing open the doors to the small houses and overturning the stalls as they searched impatiently beneath them, plainly intent on finding something or someone!

The earlier atmosphere of relaxed happiness had gone and instead the alleyway and the people in it had become a place of sharply raised voices and almost palpable fear.

A large four-wheel-drive vehicle with blacked out windows came tearing down the alleyway, sending people scattering, and then screeching to a halt. The uniformed man who got out was heavily guarded and Katrina drew in a small gasp of breath as she recognised Zuran's Minister of Internal Affairs, the cousin of Zuran's ruler himself.

Apprehensively she looked at her captor, torn between conflicting emotions. She had seen him enter the building across the alleyway dressed as a Tuareg tribesman, and his behaviour was hardly that of a man with nothing to hide. By rights she should at the very least draw the attention of the fearsome heavily armed men swarming the alleyway to his presence and her own suspicions, but... But what? But he possessed a dangerous fascination that was seducing her into... Into what? Determinedly she started to pull away from him. He checked her small movement immediately, not merely tightening his hold on her, but actually dragging her further back into a narrow space in the shadows of the alley, which was so confined that she was pressed right up against his body.

'Look, I don't know what's going on, but—' she began bravely.

'Quiet.' The icy, emotionless command was whispered against her ear. She told herself that the reason her own body was trembling so violently was because she was shocked and afraid; nothing to do with the fact that she was sharply aware of the male hardness of the muscular thigh pressing into her. And the heavy thump of the male heart was beating so strongly that it seemed to pound, not just through his body, but through her own as well, overriding the shallow beat of her own heart, overwhelming her with its life force, making her feel as though his heart were providing the life force for both of them.

The sudden echo of an old, sharp pain speared her. Her parents' love for one another had been like that: total and all-encompassing, and for ever.

She made a small sound, an incoherent murmur of private emotional angst, but his reaction was swift and punitive.

His hand gripped her throat, his head blotted out the street, and his mouth silenced any protest she could have made even before she had thought to take the breath to make it.

He tasted of heat and the desert, and a thousand and one things that had been imprinted on him, and which were alien to her. Alien and somehow dangerously and erotically exciting, she recognised in self-disgust as against her will an uncheckable surge of primitive female reaction seized her body.

Her lips softened and parted. She felt his missed heartbeat and then the sledgehammer blow of recognition that followed it as he seized like a predator the advantage she had given him. The hard pressure of his mouth on hers increased and fire jolted through her as his tongue thrust fiercely against her own, demanding her compliance.

Her body shook with reaction. Never, ever had she envisaged that she would kiss a man with such intimate sensuality in public and in full daylight, and certainly not a man who was a complete stranger to her.

She was vaguely aware of the sound of the four-wheel drive moving off, but his mouth was still covering hers.

Then, so abruptly that she almost stumbled, he released her. One hand steadied her with a merciless lack of emotion and then he was gone, disappearing into the crowd, leaving her feeling overwhelmed and, more shockingly, as though she had been abandoned.

'Your Highness…' Low, respectful bows followed his swift progress through his older half-brother's royal palace as he made his way to his presence.

The armed guards on duty outside the heavy gold-leaf-covered double doors that led to the Ruler's formal audience room threw both doors open and then bowed and left.

Xander was now in his half-brother's presence, and so he bowed deeply as the doors closed behind him. They might share the same father, his elder brother might have a well-known fondness for him, but the man in front of him was Zuran's ruler, and in public at least respect had to be paid to that fact.

Immediately the Ruler stood up and then commanded Xander to rise and come forward to embrace him.

'It is good to have you back. I have heard excellent

things about you from other world leaders, little brother, and from our embassies in America and Europe.'

'You are too kind, Your Highness. All such credit must go to you in deigning to honour me with the task of ensuring that our embassies have the personnel they need in order to promote your plans for greater democracy.'

Without any command needing to be given a door opened and a servant appeared, followed by two more bringing fragrantly fresh coffee.

Both men waited until the small ceremony had been completed.

As soon as they were alone the Ruler walked over to Xander.

'Come, let us walk in the garden.' He told him, 'We can talk more easily there.'

Beyond the audience room and screened from it by a heavy curtain lay a lushly planted private courtyard garden, alive with the sound of water from its many fountains.

Not a single speck of dust marred the perfection of the mosaic-tiled pathways as the two men walked side by side in their pristine white robes.

'It is as we suspected,' Xander announced quietly as they came to a halt in front of one of the many fishponds, and then he bent down to take a handful of food from the nearby bowl and drop it into the water.

'Nazir is plotting against you.'

'You have clear evidence of that?' the Ruler demanded sharply.

Xander shook his head. 'Not as yet. As you know,

I have managed to infiltrate and join the band of thieves and renegades led by El Khalid.'

'That traitorous wretch. I should have had him imprisoned for life instead of being so lenient with him.' The Ruler snorted.

'El Khalid has never forgiven you for depriving him of his lands and assets when you discovered his fraudulent activities. I suspect that Nazir has promised him that if he succeeds in overthrowing you he will reinstate him. I also suspect that Nazir is intending that it is El Khalid who will be seen as the one to strike against you. Of course, he himself cannot afford to be seen to be connected in any way to your assassination.' He frowned. 'You must be on your guard—'

'I am well protected, never fear, and as you say, for all that he hates me and always has done ever since we were boys, Nazir will not dare to strike openly against me.'

'It is a great pity that you cannot have him deported and banished.'

The Ruler laughed. 'No, we cannot do anything without concrete evidence, my brother. We are a democracy now, thanks in part to your own mother, but we must do everything according to the law of this land.'

His half-brother's reference to his own mother made Xander frown slightly. His mother had originally been employed as the Ruler's own governess. A passionate liberal thinker, she had taught her young pupil, and at the same time she had fallen in love with his father—a love that he had returned.

Xander himself was the result of that love, but he had never known his mother. She had died of a fever a month after his birth, having first made his father promise that he would respect her own cultural heritage in bringing up their son.

As a result of that deathbed promise, Xander had been educated in Europe and America, before being appointed as a roving Ambassador for Zuran.

'It is you who faces the greater danger, Xander,' the Ruler said warningly now. 'And, as both your brother and your ruler, I am not happy that you should be taking such a risk.'

Xander gave a small, dismissive shrug. 'We have already agreed there is no one else who we can trust implicitly and, besides, the danger is not that great. El Khalid has already accepted me in my role as a disaffected Tuareg tribesman, ostracised by his tribe for criminal activities. Indeed I have already proved my worth to him. We stopped a caravan of merchants last week and relieved them of their merchandise—'

The Ruler frowned. 'Who were they? I must see that they are recompensed, although no one has made any complaint to me of such an attack.'

'Nor will they do, I fancy,' Xander told him dryly. 'For one thing the attack took place in the empty quarter beyond Zuran's border, which is where El Khalid has his base and, for another, the merchandise we relieved them of was counterfeit currency.'

'Ah. No wonder they haven't lodged a complaint!'

'Although there have been hints and boasts from El Khalid of his involvement with some very important person, I have not as yet seen Nazir or any of his men making contact with him.

'However, if, as I suspect, Nazir plans to have you assassinated during one of your public appearances on our National Day, he will have to meet up with El

Khalid soon. Coincidentally, El Khalid has let it be known that he intends to hold an important meeting which we are all to attend, but as yet he has not said either when or where this is to be.'

'And you think that Nazir will be at this meeting?'

'Probably. I suspect his hand will be the one that guides its agenda, yes. He will want to ensure that the men chosen to accompany Khalid on an assassination mission can be relied on. Nazir won't want to risk using any of his own men, of course, so, yes, I believe he will be there. And so shall I.'

The Ruler frowned. 'You aren't concerned that Nazir may recognise you?'

'Disguised as a Tuareg?' Xander shook his head. 'I doubt it. It is after all their custom to cover their faces.'

The Ruler was still looking concerned.

'So, Highness, you are pleased then, with the progress of the new hotel complex development? I heard much praise of our country's existing tourism facilities whilst I was visiting our embassies,' Xander announced smoothly, looking warningly at his half-brother as he caught the soft sound of someone walking quietly towards them.

The greenery parted to reveal the small but powerfully stocky figure of the man they had just been discussing coming towards them, his fingers covered in heavy jewel-encrusted rings, his venomous glance resting resentfully first on Xander and then on the Ruler himself. Ignoring Xander completely, he bowed stiffly to the Ruler.

'Nazir.' The Ruler greeted him coolly. 'What brings you here? It's not often you can spare the time from your duties as our Minister of Internal Affairs to visit us socially.'

'I am extremely busy, it is true!' Nazir responded self-importantly.

'I hear there was some trouble earlier in the souk,' Xander murmured.

Immediately Nazir shot him a suspicious look. 'It was nothing… A petty thief was causing some disruption, that is all.'

'A petty thief? But you were there yourself!'

'I happened to be in the area. Besides, what business is it of yours how I conduct my duties?'

'None, other than that of a concerned citizen,' Xander answered him blandly.

His mouth compressing, Nazir turned away from him, deliberately keeping his back to him as he addressed the Sheikh. 'I understand, Your Highness, that you have ignored my advice and that you are choosing not to have the armed escort of my personal guard to ensure your safety during the National Day celebrations.'

'I am most grateful to you for your concern, cousin, but we must remember at all times our duty to the people. Our guests from other nations—especially those we hope will support our growing tourist industry—will not be reassured as to the stability of our country if they think that its ruler cannot go amongst his own people on such a joyful occasion without a phalanx of armed guards.'

'And then, of course,' Xander drawled *sotto voce* into the tension-filled silence that followed the Ruler's gentle words, 'one must always wonder *who guards the guards…*?'

A murderous look of hatred crossed Nazir's face. 'If you are suggesting—' he began savagely.

'I am suggesting nothing.' Xander stopped him coldly. 'I am merely stating fact.'

'Fact?'

'It is already proven that the presence of heavily armed personnel can lead to relatively small incidents getting completely out of hand.

'I'm sure that none of us wants to have to explain to the ambassador from another nation that one of their nationals has been shot to death by an over-enthusiastic and under-trained guard.'

'We will talk of this again, cousin, in private,' Nazir informed the Ruler grimly, pointedly ignoring Xander as he bowed briefly and left.

The Sheikh frowned as he exchanged looks with his younger half-brother.

'Our cousin forgets what is due to you, Xander,' he said angrily.

Xander gave a dismissive shrug. 'He has never hidden the fact that he has no liking for me, or my mother.'

'And your father? Our father was the greatest ruler this country has ever had! Nazir would do well to remember that! Nazir was unkind to you when you were a small child, I know, Xander, and neither I nor my father knew of his cruelty towards you then.'

'I learned to deal with it and with him.'

'Both he and his father hated your mother. They resented the influence she had over my father. And then when he made her his wife…'

'He might dislike me, but it is you he wishes to overthrow,' Xander pointed out dryly before adding, 'I have to return to the desert before my absence causes any comment. I was concerned earlier that Nazir might have become suspicious of me after he had his men turn the souk upside down looking for me, but I have learned since that it was another Tuareg they were looking for!'

'The official story is that you have only returned to Zuran briefly and are leaving the country again tonight to enjoy a well deserved rest. It is a pity you do not have time, though, to look over our new joint ventures. Your mares have produced a handsome crop of new foals, and the first phase of the marina development is approaching completion.'

Xander smiled a flash of strong white teeth against the golden honey of his skin.

The Ruler was famous throughout the world for his involvement in the world of horse racing.

As they turned to walk back to the palace the Ruler turned towards him. 'I am not sure that I should be allowing you to do this, you know,' he told him seriously. 'You are very dear to me, my little brother. Even dearer than you know. Your mother was the closest I had to a mother myself. She opened my mind to a wealth of knowledge. It was her influence on our father that led to him thinking about the long-term future of our country and when she died I believe he himself lost the will to live. I have lost both of them, little brother. I do not wish to lose you.'

'Nor I you,' Xander answered him steadily as they embraced one another.

'Hello there, beautiful! How about coming out with me tonight? I hear that His Highness is holding a very grand reception to celebrate the start of the racing season, and then afterwards we could go on to a club.'

The light-hearted invitation she was being given by the group's bachelor photographer made Katrina smile. Tom Hudson was an unashamed and incorrigible flirt, but one could not help but like him.

She started to shake her head, sunlight bouncing off the soft waves of her shoulder-length hair, but before she could say anything Richard broke in sharply.

'We are all here to work, and not to socialise, and you would do well to remember that, Hudson. Besides, we've got an early start in the morning,' he reminded them.

In the uncomfortable silence that followed the expedition leader's outburst, Tom pulled a wry face at Richard behind his back.

For all that he was very highly qualified, Richard was not popular with any of them, although it was Katrina who suffered most from his presence.

'He's gruesome,' Beverley Thomas, the only other female member of the group, commented later, giving a small shudder as she sat on the edge of Katrina's bed.

The luxurious private villa that had been put at the team's disposal was built on traditional lines, with the women's quarters apart from those of the men, and additional staff accommodation.

At first it had bemused Katrina to discover that she and Bev were to be locked into their quarters at night, but now in view of unwanted advances from Richard she was heartily glad of the fact that they were expected to adopt the country's customs.

'I can't help feeling sorry for his wife,' Katrina admitted.

'Mmm, me too! Not that he likes us mentioning

her. You do realise that he's well on the way to developing an obsession with you, don't you?'

When she saw the apprehensive look Katrina was giving her she relented a little and added, 'Well, perhaps calling it an obsession is going a bit too far, but he's certainly determined to get you into his bed.'

'He might want to but he's not going to,' Katrina assured her determinedly. 'I could cope with his unwanted advances, Bev, but it's when he starts using his position as expedition leader to punish me for rejecting him that I start to worry. This is my first job and I'm only on probation.'

'Try not to let him get to you,' Beverley advised her, stifling a yawn. 'I'm off to bed. It's been a long day and, as dear old Richard reminded us, we've got a pre-dawn start in the morning.'

Katrina smiled. Personally she was looking forward to their expedition into the desert to examine one of the area's desert ridges known as wadis.

She should be sleeping. It was over an hour since she had come to bed but every time she closed her eyes she was confronted with a disturbing mental image of the man with the golden eyes, as she had privately nicknamed him.

And it wasn't just the colour of his eyes that was imprinted on her memory. Her body quivered as fiercely and delicately as though strong fingers had plucked a single chord on a lyre.

This was ridiculous, she told herself stoutly. A woman of twenty-four with a doctorate in biochemistry could not submit herself to some foolish, primitive sexual response to a complete stranger. And not just a stranger, but very probably a criminal as well!

But her fingertips were already investigating the smooth curve of her mouth, restlessly seeking the imprint of his on hers. Her memory was faultlessly replaying to her everything that she had felt beneath the hard domination of his kiss.

Angrily she tried to deny what she was feeling. Her parents had been a pair of highly qualified scientists totally devoted to one another; they had lived for one another and died with one another when they'd been killed after the site they had been excavating had collapsed on them.

She had been seventeen at the time. Not a child any more, but not an adult either. Her parents, both only children, had had no other family, and their deaths had not only orphaned her but left her both with an aching need for someone to love her, someone to complete her, and with a deep-rooted fear of those feelings and the vulnerability they created within her.

Because of that she had buried them very deep inside herself, too immature and too frightened to cope with them. Instead she had concentrated on her studies, cautiously allowing herself to make friends, but not allowing anyone to get too close.

At twenty-four she had considered herself to be reasonably well adjusted and emotionally mature, but now… It was most definitely neither well adjusted nor emotionally mature to feel the way she did about a stranger.

Let's analyse this, she told herself determinedly.

You are in a different country with different customs; a country, moreover, that has always fascinated you, which is why you were so keen to come here, why you learned Zuranese in the first place.

Additionally you were on an adrenalin high brought on by an automatic fight or flight response to an unfamiliar situation. Of course such a highly charged situation was bound to affect you.

To the extent that she responded physically to a man she didn't know? A man she obviously should have been on her guard against?

Everyone was entitled to one little mistake, she tried to comfort herself. And, after all, it was extremely unlikely that she would ever see him again. She didn't want to accept how much that knowledge depressed her.

CHAPTER TWO

THE sun was just starting to rise over the horizon as they drove out of the villa in a convoy of sturdy, well-equipped four-wheel-drive vehicles heading for the desert. To Katrina's dismay, Richard had insisted that she was to travel on her own with him in the vehicle that he was driving.

'You'll be much more comfortable here with me in the lead vehicle,' he told her, laughing as he added unkindly, 'The others will all be choking on our dust.'

It was true that the speed at which he was driving was throwing up a heavy cloud of fine sand, but Katrina would still far rather have been with someone else.

'Why don't you relax and close your eyes?' Richard suggested oilily. 'Catch up on your sleep. It's going to be a long drive. But drink some water first. You know the rules about making sure we don't get dehydrated.'

Obediently she took the open bottle of water he was handing her and drank from it.

Perhaps it would be a good idea to try to sleep, Katrina acknowledged fifteen minutes or so later as she stifled a yawn and then gave in to a sudden over-whelming temptation to close her eyes. If only so that she could avoid having to make conversation with Richard. And she did feel extraordinarily sleepy. Probably because she had spent far too much of the night thinking about the man with the golden eyes. As she drifted off to sleep she felt the vehicle start to pick up speed.

It was the late afternoon sun that finally woke her as it shone in through the windscreen. The realisation of how long she had been asleep made her sit bolt upright in her seat and turn to Richard in consternation.

'You should have woken me,' she told him. 'How much longer will it be before we reach the wadi?'

It was several seconds before Richard answered her, the look in his eyes as he turned his head towards her making her feel sharply apprehensive. 'We aren't going to the wadi,' he replied smugly. 'We are going somewhere much more secluded and romantic… Somewhere where I can have you all to myself. Somewhere where I can show you…teach you…'

Katrina stared at him in dismay, hoping that she had misunderstood him, but it was obvious from the look on his face that she had not.

'Richard, you simply can't behave like this! We have to go to the wadi. The others will be expecting us…'

'They think that we've had to turn back,' he announced calmly. 'I told them that you weren't feeling very well. It was a good idea, I think, to get you to drink that water, which had some sleeping tablets in it.'

Katrina stared at him in horror.

'Richard, this is ridiculous. I'm going to telephone the others right now and—'

'You can't do that, I'm afraid.' He gave her a self-satisfied smile. 'I've got your mobile. I took it out of your bag when I stopped to tell the others we were turning back.'

Katrina couldn't believe what she was hearing.

'This is crazy! Let's just go and join the others and forget—'

'No!' He silenced her passionately. 'We are going to the oasis. I've been planning how to get you to myself for days, and this is the perfect opportunity and the oasis is the perfect place. It is in the empty quarter of the desert, a veritable no man's land, and this should appeal to you, Katrina, with your love of this region's history. It was once used as a stopping-off place by the camel trains.'

Katrina stared at him. Her throat had gone dry and her heart was thudding uncomfortably hard with apprehension. It wasn't that she was frightened of Richard exactly, but there was no denying that his behaviour pointed uncomfortably towards, if not an obsession with her, then certainly an unpleasant and unwanted preoccupation with her, just as Bev had shrewdly suspected.

'Look, there's the oasis,' Richard declared unnecessarily as the dusty track wound between a rocky outcrop revealing a clutch of palm trees and other vegetation, beyond which lay the blue shimmer of water.

As Richard stopped the vehicle Katrina acknowledged that in different circumstances—very different circumstances—she would have been entranced and fascinated by her surroundings.

The vegetation surrounding the oasis was unexpectedly lush and thick, especially on its far bank. At one time surely a river must have run here, for what else could have carved a path through the steep rocky escarpment on the other side of the oasis? Perhaps even a waterfall had plunged down the smooth, sheer rock face.

Certainly there must be an underground spring filling the oasis itself, or perhaps an underground river. But, undeniably beautiful though the oasis and its surroundings were, Katrina had no wish to remain there on her own with Richard.

Somehow she doubted that he would be responsive to any attempt from her to persuade him to abandon his plans, which meant that if she was to escape she would have to find a way to distract him long enough to allow her to get her hands on the vehicle's keys and drive off in it before Richard could stop her.

'I've brought a tent with me and everything else we will need.'

'Oh, how clever of you!' Katrina told him, trying to sound impressed. 'I'll stay here, shall I, whilst you unpack everything?'

Richard shook his head at her.

'No, I'm afraid you can't do that, my dear! I haven't gone to all this trouble to have you do something silly like trying to run away from me!'

He couldn't *make* her move, Katrina comforted herself, but a few seconds later, after she had told him quietly that she was not prepared to get out of the vehicle, she realised she had under-estimated the lengths he was prepared to go to.

'Well, in that case, my dear, I'm afraid you leave me no option but to use these.' He reached into his pockets and produced a pair of handcuffs. 'I really wish it wasn't necessary to do this, but if you refuse to do as I ask then I am going to have to handcuff you to the door of the vehicle.'

She had been wrong not to feel afraid of him,

Katrina acknowledged as a cold sweat broke out on her skin. He had already locked the doors of the vehicle and if she allowed him to handcuff her inside it then she'd be trapped.

'It would be nice to have some fresh air,' she conceded, trying to keep her voice steady. 'Perhaps I could sit by the oasis whilst you unpack everything?'

'Of course you can, my dear,' Richard agreed, smiling at her. 'Let's go and find somewhere comfortable for you, shall we?'

She mustn't give up hope, Katrina told herself stoutly five minutes later. Richard was escorting her to the oasis, his behaviour more that of a jailer than a would-be lover.

'This will do,' he announced, indicating one of the palm trees, but as Katrina walked towards it he held back. When she caught the warning chink of metal on metal she knew immediately that it was the handcuffs he had shown her earlier. Without stopping to think, she started to run, her flight from him as panic-stricken as that of a delicately boned gazelle. Fear drove her forward, towards the narrow pass between the steep rocks, oblivious to the sound of vehicles being driven fast over the bumpy terrain and the cries of warrior horsemen. Too late to realise what those sounds were, she burst through the pass and into full view of the group of fugitives.

They were led by El Khalid, but it was one of his young lieutenants who saw her first. He swerved the battered Land Rover he was driving round so hard that he almost overturned it.

Behind Katrina, at the pass between the rocks, Richard fell back in terror, and then turned and ran towards his own vehicle, ignoring Katrina's plight. He leapt into it and started the engine, driving back in the direction he had come as fast as he could.

Katrina, though, was oblivious to his desertion of her.

The air around her was thick with choking dust, the last dying rays of the sun striking blindingly against the metal of the vehicle racing alongside her. The driver was leaning out of the window, one hand on the steering wheel, the other reaching for her, a lascivious grin slicing his face.

Immediately she turned to run back the way she had come. Unwanted though Richard's attentions were, she could deal far more easily with him than she could with what she was now facing, but to her horror she recognised that her escape route was already being blocked off by the horse and rider bearing down on her even as she still tried to run from him.

The sound of his horse's hooves mingled with the fierce cries of the men surrounding her. He was so close to her that she could feel the heat of the horse's breath on her skin. Her heart felt as though it were about to burst. She saw him draw level with her and bend low in his saddle, his hand coming out, and then unbelievably she was being lifted off the ground and swept up onto the horse's back in front of him, as his prisoner.

Sobbing for breath, her heart pounding sickly, her face pressed against the coarsely woven cloth of the tunic he was wearing, she could do nothing other than lie there, forced to breathe in the smell of the fabric, with its faint lemony scent. Katrina stiffened. She now realised the lemony cologne, like the scent of the man himself, were both immediately familiar to her.

The drumming of horse's hooves became the drumming of her own heart as she struggled to twist her body so that she could look up into his face.

As she had expected all she could see of it were his eyes—gold-flecked, reminding her of a tiger's eye. Her heart leapt and banged against her chest wall as she looked into them and saw them flash gold sparks of molten anger back at her.

Quickly she turned her head, too shocked to withstand the contempt in his eyes. In the distance she could see the four-wheel drive disappearing as Richard drove himself to safety, having left her to her fate. Tears welled in her eyes and one rolled down her face to land on the golden warmth of the male hand holding the horse's reins.

His mouth hardening, he shook it away. He murmured to the horse as he wheeled round and started to head back to the group of men watching them.

As he did so out of nowhere, or so it seemed to Katrina, a vehicle appeared, driven at frightening speed right at them. In the driver's seat was the man who had first pursued her, his face contorted with savagery as he shook his fist at her captor and mouthed some words in a dialect she could not understand before driving off again, reaching the waiting onlookers ahead of them.

There were a hundred, no, a thousand questions she wanted to ask, Katrina acknowledged, but before she could do so he was reining in his mount in front of a powerfully built man of medium height, who was gesturing to him to dismount.

Katrina shivered to see the powerful-looking rifle he was wearing slung over one shoulder, an ammunition belt around his waist, into which was thrust a wicked-looking traditionally curved dagger.

At his side was the man who had pursued her, gesticulating angrily as he pointed towards her and burst into a rapid speech, of which she could only catch the odd word.

A brief inclination of his head from the man at her side told Katrina that the man with the gun must be the leader of the men. But whilst he obviously commanded the obedience of everyone else, she was aware that her captor's body language was subtly emphasising his own independence.

'Why did you let the man get away?' Katrina heard the leader demand angrily in Zuranese.

There was a brief pause before her captor answered him coolly, 'El Khalid, you're asking me a question you should surely be asking another! A man on horseback, even when that animal is as fast as any mount in the Ruler's fabled stable, cannot hope to outrun a four-wheel drive. Sulimen could have caught up with him had he not decided to pursue an easier prey.'

'He has taken my prize and now he seeks to discredit me. The girl is mine, El Khalid,' the driver of the Land Rover protested hotly.

'You hear what Sulimen says, Tuareg! What do you answer him?'

Katrina had to bite down hard on her lip to stop herself from turning to her captor and begging him not to let Sulimen take her. The leader had called him 'Tuareg', using only his tribal name, whereas he had used the more intimate Sulimen for the other man. Did that mean he would favour the other's claim? Katrina felt sick at the thought.

Why didn't her captor say something...? She could

feel him looking at her, but she could not bring herself to lift her head and look back at him. She was
too afraid of what she might see in his eyes.

'I answer him that I have the girl and he does not.
She will earn me a fat purse when I take her back to
Zuran City and ransom her back to her people.'

'No one is to leave this camp until I say so,' came
the harsh response. 'I have gathered you all here in
this place for a special mission. Our success in it will
make us all very rich men.

'Since both of you lay claim to the girl, then you
might fight one another for her.' He gave a small jerk
of his head, and before Katrina could protest she was
being led forcibly away by two fierce-looking armed
men.

Anxiously she turned round just in time to see El
Khalid removing the glitteringly sharp-edged hooked
dagger from his belt and throwing it towards her captor.

The breath left her lungs in a rush as he caught it
and he and Sulimen began to circle one another.
Sulimen already had a similar dagger in his hand and
almost immediately he jabbed savagely at his opponent with it. The other men had begun to form a circle
around them.

Standing behind them between her jailers, Katrina
could only catch maddeningly brief glimpses of the
two men as they fought.

Not that she liked watching men fight—far from
it—but on this occasion she had a very strong reason
for wanting to know which one was going to be the
victor. Whilst the men had dragged her away, the two
opponents, whilst retaining their headgear, had re-

moved their cloaks and tunics and were fighting bare-chested as they circled one another barefoot.

It was now dark and lanterns had been lit to illuminate the scene that to Katrina looked like something from another world.

The light from one of the lanterns glittered on the daggers as they were raised in clenched hands, and the sickening sounds of human combat echoed the thuds of bare feet on sand.

She heard a low grunt of pain and heard the watching men roar in approval; above their heads she could see the hand holding a dagger aloft, the light catching the tiny droplets of blood that fell from it. Her stomach heaved. Was the man with the golden eyes badly wounded? Ridiculously, given all she already knew about him and all that she didn't, her anxiety and concern were not for her own plight and safety, but for his, and she knew that had she been able to do so she would have rushed to his side.

She heard another groan and another roar of approval, but this time it was the name 'Tuareg' the watching men were calling out in praise.

The fight seemed to go on for ever, and Katrina was becoming increasingly sickened by the thought of such violence and cruelty. She was simply not programmed to find anything about physical violence acceptable, Katrina acknowledged. Her initial anxious need to see what was happening had been overlaid by relief that she was spared witnessing such a loathsome spectacle.

But at last it was apparently over, the watching men cheering loudly as she was pulled through their ranks to where the two antagonists stood in front of El Khalid.

Only one of the three men commanded her attention, though, and her stomach churned with a mixture of nausea and guilty relief as she heard the crowd chanting 'Tuareg' and saw that in his hands he was holding aloft both of the daggers, whilst his opponent slumped despondently beside him.

But then he turned round and Katrina sucked in a shocked breath as she saw the blood-beaded wounds on his flesh. One had slit the taut skin of his face along his cheekbone and dangerously close to his eye, another was carved just above his heart, and blood was dripping from a third on his upper arm.

A feeling of sick dizziness began to threaten her, but she ignored it, dragging her gaze away from the sweat-gilded expanse of taut male chest in front of her. Sulimen, in contrast, did not appear to have any wounds at all, which puzzled Katrina a little since 'Tuareg' was obviously the victor.

'Here is your prize,' she heard El Khalid telling him. 'Take her.'

Was it her imagination or was the slight bow her captor made in El Khalid's direction more cynical than respectful? If so, no one else seemed to have thought so.

He still hadn't so much as acknowledged her presence, turning to toss El Khalid's dagger back to him, and then turning back to lean forward and scoop up his discarded tunic.

Out of the corner of her eye Katrina saw Sulimen go to sheathe his own dagger, but then terrifyingly, instead of doing so, he lunged violently towards her captor's unprotected back, the dagger clenched in his raised hand.

Katrina heard her own sharp sound of shocked

warning, but it seemed something else must have alerted 'Tuareg' to the danger because he had already whirled round, and in a movement so fast that Katrina's eyes could not follow it he had kicked out at Sulimen's raised hand, dislodging the knife.

Immediately three men seized Sulimen and dragged him away. As though nothing at all out of the ordinary had happened, her captor picked up his tunic and pulled it on before indicating with a brusque inclination of his head that she was to join him.

'Come,' he said peremptorily. He took such long strides that she had difficulty in keeping up with him, but the moment she reached his side he stopped walking and turned to look down at her.

'You will not walk at my side, but behind me,' he told her coldly.

Katrina could hardly believe her ears. And as for walking behind him! The traumas she had endured were forgotten, in the full fury of her outraged female pride.

'I will do no such thing,' she refused hotly. 'I am not your…your chattel… And besides, in Zuran men walk alongside their partners.'

'This is not Zuran, it is the desert, and you are mine to do with as I choose, when and how I choose.'

Without giving her the opportunity to answer him, he turned away and continued to walk swiftly towards the pitched tents, which were cleverly concealed from view in a protective natural enclosure of steep-sided rocky outcrops.

Several fires had been started in a clearing in front of some of the tents and dark-robed women were stirring the contents of cooking pots. The rich smell of cooking food made Katrina realise just how long it was since she herself had eaten, and her stomach growled hungrily.

Predictably, she felt, the tent her captor had led her to was set apart from the others.

A battered-looking utility-type vehicle was parked alongside it and behind that his horse was tethered, happily munching on some food, watched over by a young boy. But Katrina wasn't given any time to study her surroundings; a hard hand in the middle of her back was already pushing her into the tent.

She had of course seen similar tents set up for display and educational purposes on a cultural education site in Zuran City, but she had never imagined she might occupy one of them! Several lamps cast a soft glow over the tent's main living area, with its richly patterned carpets and traditional divan. There were several cushions on the floor and a low wooden table with a coffee pot on it.

All at once the events of the day caught up with her and reaction swamped her, causing exhausted tears to fill her eyes.

'What are you crying for? Your lover? I doubt he is wasting any tears on you, to judge by the speed with which he abandoned you.'

Katrina stared at him. 'Richard is not my lover! He's a married man…'

'But of course. Otherwise, why would he bring you to such a remote place?' A cynical smile hardened the narrowed eyes.

'I did not allow him. He…he forced me…'

'Of course he did!' he agreed mockingly.

Katrina lifted her head and looked challengingly at him.

'Why are you pretending to be a Tuareg when it is obvious that you are not—?'

'Silence!' he commanded her angrily.

'No. I will not be silent. I remember you from the alleyway in Zuran City, even if you don't.'

She gave a small breathless gasp as his hand closed hard over her mouth, a menacing look glittering in his eyes as he bent towards her and said softly, 'You will be silent.'

Katrina had had enough! She had been kidnapped, bullied, threatened, and now this! Angrily she bit sharply into the hand covering her mouth, more shocked by the salt taste of his blood than by the savagery of the oath he uttered as he wrenched away from her.

'Woman, you are a hell-cat!' he stormed as he frowned down at the tiny pinpricks of blood on the soft pad of flesh just below his thumb. 'But no way will I allow you to poison me with your venom! Clean it.'

Katrina stared at him in disbelief, her face starting to burn. What she had done had shocked her. Outraged female fury stiffened her whole body. And yet shockingly there, deep down inside her, was a vagrant acknowledgement of intoxicatingly dangerous awareness of the sensuality of her own thoughts. Thoughts that mirrored her own actual desires? Desires she secretly wanted to turn into actions?

Absolutely not! She could feel his breath against her ear, and she took the cloth he was handing her, dipped it in the bowl of water next to her and dabbed the wound.

Abruptly he released her and stepped back from her, his voice both harsh and somehow distorted as he demanded thickly, 'No! Why should I give you the opportunity to inflict even more damage?'

'Why are you behaving like this?' Katrina demanded tremulously. 'Who are you? In the souk, you looked European.'

'You will not say such things. You know nothing about me!'

She could hear the savage rejection and hostility in his voice. 'I know that you are not a Tuareg,' she persisted.

'And you would know, of course,' he taunted her, his anger replaced by mockery.

'Yes, I would,' Katrina confirmed bravely. 'I have studied Zuranese history and culture and no true Tuareg male would ever uncover his face in public the way you did the other day in the alleyway...'

There was a small telling silence before he said quietly but oh, so menacingly, 'If I were you, I would forget all about Zuran City and its alleyways.'

Katrina took a deep breath and then exhaled it raggedly. 'So, are you going to tell me who you are?'

For a few seconds she thought he wasn't going to reply. And then he gave a small dismissive shrug. 'Who I am does not matter. But what I am does. Those of us who have given our allegiance to El Khalid have strong reasons for doing so. We live outside the law as you know it and you would do well to remember that.'

'You're a criminal?' she guessed. 'A fugitive?'

'You ask too many questions and, I can assure you, you would not want to know who and what I really am.'

It was hard not to allow herself to shiver in reaction to those menacing words, and to demand instead,

'Well, at least give me a name that I may call you. You cannot really want to be called Tuareg. I would certainly not want to be called English!'

To her astonishment he laughed.

'Very well, then. You may call me...' Xander paused. To give her his real name of Allessandro was impossible. It was far too easily recognisable. Here in the rebel camp, where a man's lawful identity was respected as his own private business, he was known by everyone only as 'Tuareg' and had given himself the very common family name of bin Sadeen. But 'Tuareg' wasn't the name he wanted to hear falling from this woman's lips, although just why he should feel like that he wasn't prepared to analyse.

'You may call me Xander,' he heard himself telling her. Xander was the shortened version of his name used only by those who were closest to him, his half-brother and sister-in-law, and so would not be recognised by anyone else.

'Xander?' A small frown etched Katrina's smooth forehead. 'That is very unusual. I do not believe I have heard it before.'

'It was my mother's choice,' he told her curtly. 'And what am I to call you?'

'My name is Katrina Blake,' she informed him, hesitating before finding the courage to burst out anxiously, 'How long will it be before...before I can go back to Zuran City?'

'I cannot say. El Khalid has given orders that no one is to leave the oasis until he permits it.'

For a moment Katrina was tempted to ask him what had brought them to the oasis, and indeed the question was already on the tip of her tongue, but cautiously she decided not to ask it.

'Very wise,' he told her coolly, as though he had guessed what she was thinking.

'Stay here,' he ordered her. 'Do not leave the tent.'

'Where are you going?' Katrina demanded wildly as he started to walk away from her.

Turning round, he told her smoothly. 'To my sleeping quarters to remove my soiled clothes.'

Oh! Katrina felt herself begin to blush.

'Oh, your cuts,' she remembered with guilt. 'Shouldn't you have them attended to?'

He shrugged carelessly. 'They are mere scratches, that is all, and will heal quickly enough.'

Katrina suddenly remembered something. 'Why was it Sulimen who lost the fight when you were the one who was injured?' she asked him curiously.

'The aim is not to carve slices from one's opponent, but to disarm him,' he told her dispassionately.

As he turned away again she looked towards the exit.

'There are two hundred miles of empty desert between here and Zuran City.'

The clinically detached words sent a tingle of apprehensive hostility and despair zinging over her skin. The desert was its own kind of prison—a guard designed by nature to prevent her from escaping him, and he of course knew that. Did he also know how afraid she had been when Sulimen had claimed her as his trophy? How relieved she had been when he had stepped in? How complex and disquieting the tangled mass of her own emotions was? Her mouth compressed. She sincerely hoped not! He was already making her feel far more emotionally vulnerable than she knew was wise.

Determinedly she turned round to confront him.

'You won't get away with this, you know. Richard will alert the authorities and—'

'We are in the empty quarter—beyond the reach of both your lover and the authorities,' he replied chillingly.

'Richard is my boss, not my lover.' Katrina's face burned as she saw the way he was looking at her.

'So why else would you be at the oasis, together and alone? Though I'm not surprised that you should deny your relationship with him after the way he has abandoned you.'

'He obviously thought it made good sense for him to go for help rather than for both of us to be taken hostage,' Katrina returned shortly.

'"Good sense"? Oh, of course, you are European!' he taunted her. 'Here in the desert it is not "good sense". We are driven by our interactions with your sex, especially when we are bound to a woman, emotionally committed to them. But then, of course, your culture does not consider such things important, does it? I would rather cut out my own heart than abandon the woman who held it to any kind of discomfort or danger.'

Something in his voice was raising goose-bumps on Katrina's skin and a dangerous burning sensation at the backs of her eyes. The intimate and intense images his words were conjuring for her were intruding on dreams she held so private and secret that just the sound of his voice was enough to bring them to the front of her mind. Hadn't she always longed for such a man and such a love and hadn't she told herself that she was hungering for something that did not exist? Hadn't she strived to make herself put aside such foolishness and to concentrate instead on the realities of life?

Swallowing hard against the ball of emotion blocking her throat, she turned away from him.

'Go if you wish,' she heard him say carelessly from behind her. 'If Sulimen does not take you, then the desert most surely will.'

Katrina made no response. How could she when she knew that he was speaking the truth?

Although she had her back to him, disconcertingly she knew immediately when he had left the living area of the pavilion and gone through to his sleeping quarters.

The rush of adrenalin that had given her the courage to speak so challengingly to him had gone and she felt weak and shaky. The pavilion and its owner were her prison and her guard, but they were also her place of safety and her protection, she acknowledged.

But she must not allow herself to forget just what he was! She could remember reading somewhere of the intense and dangerous emotional dependence a captive could end up having on his or her captor. She must not let that happen to her.

Because he had kissed her? Just because he had used her? Her head had begun to ache and she was beginning to feel slightly sick on the heavy mixture of adrenalin and anxiety unleavened by anything else.

She paced the soft carpet of the pavilion, checking and tensing at every alien sound, but she was still caught off guard when she turned round and saw that Xander had padded soft-footed into the room and was standing watching her.

He was wearing a clean soft white tunic that he was still fastening, his feet and head bare. In the lamplight she could see the golden gleam of his chest through the soft mesh of fine dark hair.

A feeling she couldn't control exploded deep down inside her body, releasing an ache so shocking and intimate that it made her catch her breath on a betraying indrawn rattle.

His hair was damp and as he walked across the carpet towards her he brought with him the smell of clean skin and the subtle cologne she was already associating with him. Her heart did a neat double somersault inside her body and then just in case she had not got the message, it took a high dive on a trapeze that left her feeling as though it had somehow become lodged in her throat.

He was making her feel uncomfortable and very aware of the difference between his clean, fresh appearance and her own tired stickiness. But even without that he was making her feel uncomfortable, full stop, Katrina acknowledged mutely. She was trying desperately to drag her traitorous gaze away from the dark hand casually fastening the robe buttons and concealing from her the matt satin gold of his bare flesh.

In an attempt to cover what she was feeling she demanded sharply, 'Just how long do you plan to keep me here?'

He shot her a look of cold arrogance. 'For as long as I have to!'

She was finding it difficult to swallow. 'What... what will you do?' Could he hear the nervousness in her voice?

He gave her a look of narrow-eyed scrutiny and then questioned mockingly, 'Do?'

'Yes. I mean—' She had to stop speaking to swallow again. 'I mean, how will you let the expedition know that—?'

'You ask far too many questions! There is a saying, isn't there, in your country about curiosity?'

'About curiosity killing the cat, you mean?' Katrina managed to croak.

'In your shoes I should concern myself more with questioning how willing your friends are to buy your freedom and at what price than how I intend to go about informing them of your whereabouts.'

Katrina could feel the panic biting into her, but she refused to give in to it. Her parents' death had forced her into self-reliance at a young age and the habit of depending on herself and facing up to sometimes very unpleasant truths and realities was one she had forced herself to adopt.

And right now there was a very unpleasant question she had to have an answer to. Moistening her over-dry lips, she pressed him huskily, 'And if my...if the company cannot pay the ransom demand?'

There was a small pause and a flash of something she couldn't interpret in his eyes before he said softly, 'Then in that case I shall have to take my goods to a wider market.' When she looked blankly at him he derided her, 'Who else will pay handsomely for a young attractive woman?'

Katrina's eyes widened as she stared at him in appalled anxiety. He couldn't mean what he was saying. Could he?

Without another word he pulled on his Tuareg headdress, slid his feet into a pair of sandals and, pulling back the heavy curtain, stepped out of the tent.

She was alone! He had gone! She could simply walk out if she wished. But walk out to what? She was pretty sure that a group of men such as these, bound together by their illegal activities, would post guards on their camp. If she tried to leave she would suffer the ignominy of being forcibly brought back, and even if she should succeed in escaping, she knew she could not possibly walk back to Zuran City. No, she had no option other than to wait tamely here, for him and whatever fate he chose to impose on her. And of course he knew that!

Whatever fate?

Supposing he himself should decide that he found her desirable? Her heart thumped heavily against her ribs, and a frisson of sensation that shamingly had nothing whatsoever to do with either fear or outrage stroked feather touches of liquid and dangerous excitement over her.

His dishonesty must obviously pay him well, she decided cynically, at least if the interior of the pavilion and its furnishings were anything to go by.

The carpets covering the floor and 'walls' were exquisitely worked and far superior to anything she had seen in the shops she had visited. She touched one of them tentatively, stroking her fingertip along one of the branches and then down the thick trunk of its richly hued tree of life. The silky threads felt as warm as though they were a living, breathing entity. If she closed her eyes she could almost imagine...

Her face was on fire as she snatched her hand back from the carpet as though she had been burned. The carved and gilded raised divan was draped with something dark and soft, jewel-coloured velvet cushions piled on top of it. The flickering oil lamps cast mysterious shadows, which echoed the sensual richness of the fabrics. A discarded lute-like instrument lay on the floor to one side of the divan, and behind them she could see a pile of leather-bound books.

Automatically she went over to them and picked one of them up. Its title was picked out in gold leaf, *The Rubaiyat of Omar Khayyam*... A book of poetry. It seemed out of character somehow. She put the book back and sat down on one of the cushions. Her head was still aching and she felt both physically and emotionally exhausted. Tiredly she closed her eyes.

Pensively Xander picked his way through the tents towards his own, pausing to check on the mare he had been riding earlier. When she saw him she tossed her head and pushed her nose into his arm, begging for the tidbit he always gave her. The boy whom he paid to keep an eye on her sprang up from where he had been lying several feet away from her and then settled down again as he recognised him.

Katrina's challenge to him about his European inheritance had rubbed against a raw place in his emotional make-up. His mother had been loved and respected by all of his Zurani family, with the exception of Nazir and Nazir's late father. And, according to his half-brother, his mother had happily embraced the way of life of her husband. She had loved the desert and its people, as he did himself, but she had not been totally and completely desert blood, bone and sinew, just as he wasn't himself. His father had chosen to have him educated in Europe, wanting him to experience his European cultural inheritance, and to keep the promise he had made to his dying wife, but Xander had never forgotten overhearing a conversation between his father and the British government official who had undertaken to escort him to his new school in England.

'The thing is that the boy is neither fish nor fowl, really…' the diplomat had announced critically, or so it had seemed to Xander's ears at that time.

And the diplomat had spoken the truth, Xander acknowledged bleakly now. Whilst the greatest part of him would always belong here in the desert, there was another part of him that felt most fulfilled when he was involved in the cut and thrust of diplomacy in Washington and London and Paris, and the work he did promoting Zuran. He had grown up surrounded by the love of his Zurani relatives, yes, but at the same time he had been aware that he was different from them. He was not European, but neither was he totally Zurani either!

And because of that, coupled no doubt with the loss of his mother, he carried with him the secret, guarded burden of his own inner sense of isolation.

But somehow Katrina had breached his defences and touched the darkness buried deep within his own soul. And because of that more than anything else he wanted her out of his life!

After all, whilst as a child he had seen his mixed heritage as a source of confusion and anxiety, as an adult he had learned to view it in a much more positive light and to use it for the benefit of others. But, even so, he was still very much aware that in some people's eyes his mixed heritage made him an object of their contempt.

With his elder half-brother's blessing he had worked tirelessly to promote better relations between his country and the rest of the world, and indeed he had been honoured for the work he had done by the

Ruling Council by being appointed as a Special Envoy. It was a scheme he had personally advocated and set up involving a student exchange between Middle Eastern and European students so that each might better understand the other, and had been so highly acclaimed that there was talk of his name being put forward for the Nobel Peace Prize.

But right now his emotions were turbulent rather than peaceful! And all because of Katrina Blake! Of all the complications and problems he could have envisaged that might jeopardise his carefully made plans, the unexpected and unwanted presence of Katrina Blake was surely the last one he could have logically expected. It was certainly the last one he wanted, he acknowledged savagely. And definitely the last one he had been prepared for! She was a danger, both to him and to herself! By rights, surely the situation she was in should have caused her to be struck dumb with fear, not bombarding him with questions. And certainly not making her observations and information about him common knowledge. Potentially she could ruin everything! She was a liability he could not afford to have, here where she could threaten and unwittingly sabotage his own secret mission. But El Khalid had given the edict that no one was to leave the camp. Otherwise he could have driven her safely out of the way, radioed ahead and got a car and a driver to pick her up and take her back to her friends—and her laggardly cowardly lover—and then been left unencumbered to return here to do what he had come here to do.

Instead of which…

He should have left her to fate and to Sulimen, he decided bitterly. Reluctantly he found himself acknowledging that she had spirit and courage. And she had a mouth that smelled of scented damask roses and tasted of honey-drenched almonds. Her body was as slender as a young gazelle's and her eyes...

He wrenched his thoughts back under control. His half-brother's wife had introduced any number of suitable young women to him as potential brides but none of them had interested him. They had been too sweet, too docile, too lacking in spirit. Soft, tame doves, who would flutter to any man's hand, where something in him craved a little of the proud independence, the desert wildness of the she falcon, who would only allow herself to be tamed by one man— and even then only on her own terms.

A woman who would melt into his arms in a sweetly wild passion, which would meet and match his own fiercely strong male hunger for her. A woman who would give herself to him body and soul and who would demand from him in return all that there was of him. A woman who would race him neck and neck across the desert sands and who would place her head upon his lap whilst he played music for her and read her the sweetest and most tender of love poems. A woman who was all that he had been told his own mother had been and yet who at the same time was individually and uniquely herself.

He had long ago decided that such a woman could not and did not exist, outside his own imagination, and he still thought that, he told himself fiercely. Katrina Blake certainly wasn't such a woman. How could she be?

And more importantly by far: how could he be wasting time thinking about her when his thoughts and his energies should be focused on much more important matters? He was as sure as he could be that the important personage El Khalid had spoken of had to be Nazir.

Even though he had tried discreetly to persuade El Khalid to be more specific about when he was expecting the important person to arrive, the rebel leader had insisted that a definite time had not yet been arranged, and Xander had been reluctant to push El Khalid too hard for information in case he began to suspect his motives.

Nazir could not afford to delay too long. The celebration of the country's National Day was only five days away, after all. And Nazir certainly would not welcome Katrina's presence within the camp—a woman who, if she chanced to see him, could potentially betray him if she was returned to her own people. Indeed, from Nazir's point of view it would be far simpler and safer if she did not return!

The smell of cooking food reminded him that he had not had anything to eat. Going over to the communal fire, he helped himself to a plate of lamb stew from the pot and then picked up some of the flat unleavened bread.

CHAPTER THREE

THE first thing Xander saw when he swept aside the heavy curtain and walked into the pavilion was Katrina, lying fast asleep on one of the cushions, her face pale with exhaustion and her lashes lying in delicately curled twin black semi-circles against her skin.

He started to frown. Her hair, which had been caught back, had started to escape and several tendrils clung to the exposed curve of her throat. Such a pretty colour couldn't possibly be natural, Xander decided contemptuously, and would no doubt be as false as everything else about her, right down to the lie she had told him about being forced to come to the oasis.

His frown deepened. If she continued to sleep lying the way she was she would end up with cramped muscles and a stiff neck. He put the food he was carrying down on the table and went over to her, hunkering down beside her.

His mother had been very pale skinned and fair-haired, which was no doubt why his own skin was warmly golden rather than teak brown. His mother had loved his father passionately and he her, at least according to his half-brother, and he had no reason to doubt him.

The angle of Katrina's sleeping body revealed the softly rounded curves of her breasts beneath the short-sleeved round-necked shirt she was wearing. He could see where the fabric of her shirt pulled slightly to reveal the soft thrust of her nipples. His stomach muscles contracted sharply, the pressure of his fierce attempt to quell his body's fierce surging reaction to her causing the air to squeeze out of his lungs.

He had seen plenty of nubile young women dressed far more revealingly and provocatively—and not just on the streets of the European cities he had visited—without ever feeling even the slightest twinge of sexual reaction, and it both disturbed and infuriated him that he should be so immediately and intensely aroused now and by a woman he had no business allowing himself to feel such a physical reaction to.

He was not, after all, some sexually deprived teenager! And far from inexperienced! If he wanted a woman there were any number who would be all too eager to share his bed. Any number maybe, but what about this particular one? She was another man's lover. A married man's lover, he reminded himself.

Broodingly he looked down at Katrina, his intellect rejecting the message his body was giving him, and the urge to simply pick her up and carry her into the inner privacy of his sleeping quarters.

She moved her head and a thick lock of her hair fell across her face, making her frown in her sleep. Automatically he reached out to brush it away for her.

Abruptly Katrina opened her eyes, her heart hammering frantically fast inside her chest as she looked up into the molten gold of Xander's fiercely predatory gaze. Helplessly she lay motionless and vulnerable beneath it, pinioned by it, her lips parting as she took short gulps of air.

His fingertips were touching her cheek, four cool, hard pressure points, each one sending shock waves of pleasure that were making her tremble. She could see the dark shadow along his jaw, her eyes widening in betraying female acknowledgement of its message of maleness.

Immediately he lifted his hand from her face, something dark and dangerous glittering in his eyes before he veiled his expression from her.

'I have brought you some food,' he told her curtly.

Katrina could smell it, and her stomach rumbled hungrily, but she compressed her mouth and shook her head, telling him untruthfully, 'I'm not hungry.'

He was frowning as he looked at her.

'Liar,' he said to her flatly, before demanding coldly, 'What is it? Is our food not good enough for you?'

'No, it isn't that!'

'No? Then what exactly is it?' he challenged her sardonically.

'I...Richard—'

'Richard? Your lover, you mean?'

'He is not my lover. He wanted to be, but I... He tricked me and...and drugged me...'

'Drugged you? And you think I might do the same?'

She had angered him; she could tell that!

'Why should I want to do that?'

Stubbornly Katrina refused to answer him.

'Are you really suggesting that I would drug you in order to have sex with you?'

Katrina's face burned.

Put like that it did sound far-fetched, especially when one look at him would tell any fully functioning woman that making love with him would be all pleasure and no penance!

'Even so! Isn't it normally the custom for desert tribesmen to eat first, before their women?'

'Their women? But you are not my woman, are you?' he pointed out softly. 'And we also have a custom that a guest is invited to eat first.'

'But I am not your guest.' Katrina couldn't help answering him sharply. 'I am your prisoner!'

Picking up the stew, he sat down cross-legged on the divan and began to dip a piece of bread into it, scooping up chunks of delicious-smelling lamb.

Katrina's mouth watered. She felt faint with hunger. Pausing between mouthfuls, he demanded brusquely, 'Tell me more about this lover of yours. This Richard…'

'He is not my lover!' Katrina denied angrily. 'I have told you that already.'

'But you agreed to accompany him into the desert…alone…'

'No! It was an expedition—several of us… We are cataloguing the flora and fauna of the area. Richard tricked me into getting into his vehicle, and then…'

Against her will she could feel her own emotions threatening to overwhelm her.

'By the time I realised what he was planning it was too late. When he stopped at the oasis I hoped that I might be able to distract him and escape.'

'Distract him? In what manner? No, I can guess. There is after all only one reliable method by which a woman can distract a man.'

Katrina had had enough!

'You're as bad as Richard! You just don't understand! Believe what you like, I don't care.'

'And neither do I. At least not so far as your sexual history is concerned. What I do care about, however, is your financial value to me.' He stood up and started to walk determinedly towards her.

A sharp thrill of fear seized her. Apprehensively Katrina looked towards the door, but he was standing between her and it.

'Here.' He told her curtly, handing her the bowl of stew. 'It is not drugged. Now sit down and eat!'

Relief filled her. For a moment she had feared... She knew not what she had feared, only that she had been afraid! But it seemed that after all there was a kinder, more compassionate side to her captor!

The stew was every bit as good as it had looked, and she was even hungrier than she had known.

When she had finished Xander told her coolly, 'I have some business I need to discuss with El Khalid, and my horse to see to, but first I will show you where you will sleep.'

She was so tired she could hardly keep her eyes open, never mind follow Xander as he swung back the heavy fabric hanging that separated the outer compartment of the tent from the inner one, and she stumbled exhaustedly after him.

It took her eyes several seconds to adjust to the shadowy darkness of the inner chamber, and its low, wide bed heaped with cushions.

'Through here you will find a shower and—'

'A shower!' Her voice betrayed both her surprise and her relief. The thought of water on her dusty skin was a wonderful prospect, but it was not enough to completely distract her from the sight of the large bed. Quite obviously it was her captor's bed!

But he was already turning away from her and before she could say anything he had gone, leaving her alone in the shadowy darkness of the dimly lit chamber. Warily she started to investigate her surroundings. The bed was easily large enough for two people, and the discovery of the portable shower and loo, which lay in their own tented area beyond it and which, whilst very simple, were immaculately clean, made her exhale a gusty sigh of relief.

Since she was not sure how long Xander would be gone and, therefore, how much privacy she would have, she showered quickly, hesitating a little before wrapping her wet body in one of the obviously luxurious and expensive thick towels she had found neatly stacked on a hanging shelf. Were they someone else's property? Property which had been acquired by theft? It was hard for her to ignore her moral disquiet about using them, but she had no alternative other than to do so, she told herself grimly before fastidiously rinsing out her underwear and tee shirt.

By the time she had done all that it was all she could do to find the energy to crawl onto the bed still wrapped in her towel.

Virtually all the members of the band of renegades who had associated themselves with El Khalid were already waiting for him to begin his evening council when Xander joined them and found a space to sit down cross-legged amongst them.

'You are late, Tuareg,' one of them commented.

'He was probably too busy enjoying his prize,' another joined in coarsely, before adding in warning, 'You had best be on your guard, Tuareg. Sulimen is making no secret of the fact that he believes that the girl is rightfully his and that he wants her back.'

Xander gave a dismissive shrug.

'Sulimen may make as many empty threats as he wishes, the girl stays with me. Has El Khalid spoken yet of this mysterious personage of importance who is to make us all wealthy?' he demanded.

The other men shook their heads, and then fell silent as El Khalid himself appeared from within his large pavilion, flanked by his lieutenants.

Two hours later although many questions had been asked El Khalid had still not informed them of the identity of the man they had come to the oasis to meet, and Xander suspected that he did not as yet know Nazir's true identity himself.

It was gone midnight when the meeting broke up, and Xander made his way slowly back to his own tent, pausing only to check up on his horse and the sleeping boy who looked after her.

The boy was an orphan who had attached himself to El Khalid's camp. When all this was over he would ask his half-brother to find him a bed, an education and a job in his stables, Xander decided.

Once inside the pavilion, he removed his mobile phone from his pocket and switched it on. He had deliberately cleared it of any information that might betray him, and he dialled his half-brother's private number quickly, whilst he faced the entrance to the tent, just in case anyone should decide to enter.

'Little brother!'

He could hear the pleasure in his half-brother's voice, and quickly filled him in with what had been happening, using the special code they had arranged.

'You may have been informed of the kidnap of a certain young British woman, a member of an explorative scientific expedition,' he added carefully.

'I have heard of such an incident,' the Ruler agreed equally carefully. 'The head of the expedition has informed us that it took place in the desert some thirty or so miles to the east of our city, and a search is to be made in that area.'

Xander frowned. The oasis was over two hundred miles north of the city, which meant that Richard had lied about where he and Katrina had been when she had been 'kidnapped'.

'The girl is safe—no thanks to the one who placed her in danger. And I shall ensure that she remains so,' Xander informed his half-brother, before they ended the call. Richard might have desired Katrina, but he certainly could not have had any genuine love for her, Xander decided with angry contempt. His hostility towards the other man had grown with every damning word his half-brother had spoken. Not that he believed for one minute the wild fiction Katrina had invented about Richard tricking her into accompanying him. She was no sheltered, inexperienced girl after all, but a travelled and independent young woman who had no doubt long ago lost count of the number of men who had shared her bed.

But that did not make her deserving of the fate that would have been hers if Sulimen had been allowed to claim her.

He hadn't really needed the information relayed to him earlier by his fellows that Sulimen had a weakness for young women and he had a reputation too for treating them very badly. Sulimen didn't just want Katrina for the purpose of ransoming her, that he was sure about…

Xander's mouth compressed. She might be an unwanted complication that he could well do without, but there was no way he could abandon her to

Sulimen. As she was a stranger in his country and a woman, he had a moral duty to protect her.

His half-brother had informed him during their telephone conversation that Nazir had let it be known that he was about to leave the country for several weeks. They had both agreed that this was merely an alibi he had created, which would not only enable him to meet and plot with El Khalid, but also to mastermind his planned coup without attracting suspicion to himself.

With the Ruler's sons being under age and too young to step into their father's shoes once Nazir had disposed of him, Nazir was no doubt planning to lay claim to the throne by means of suggesting himself as Regent. Therefore, he would not want the Ruling Council to suspect what he had done.

Nazir would leave it as long as he dared before putting his plan to El Khalid in order to lessen the risk of someone betraying it and him, but he would have to make his move soon.

As he walked into the sleeping area of the pavilion, Xander started to remove his Tuareg headdress, smoothly unwinding the yards of indigo-dyed fabric that comprised it and provided him with his disguise.

Katrina had been both right and wrong in accusing him of not being Tuareg—his father did have some Tuareg blood.

Katrina. Her name had a special melody to it, a musical harmony that fell sweetly on the ear. A poet…a lover might be tempted to use it to write of his love for her. A poet? A lover? Long ago as a callow youth, he might have believed himself to have the soul of a poet, but he was most certainly not the latter. And did not want to be?

Casting aside the indigo fabric, he strode towards the bed and then stopped as he saw Katrina lying where she had fallen asleep on top of it. Her head lay on one of its silk-covered cushions; her body was wrapped in a towel that revealed more of her than it concealed, fully exposing the slender length of her legs with their creamy thighs and delicately boned ankles, so fine he suspected he could have circled one with one hand. An equally delicately boned arm was flung out to one side of her, the other tucked beneath her. She looked more child than woman, at least until one moved closer as he had just done and saw what he had not observed before, which was the upper curve of her breasts, revealed right down to the areolae surrounding her nipples and beyond them to the rosy peaked flare of the nipples themselves.

A sensation he tried savagely to repudiate exploded inside him and with it a need and a hunger that turned his eyes the colour of molten gold slashed with amber. Desire, hot, urgent and compelling, surged through him, threatening to breach his self-control.

If he touched her now he would be no better than Sulimen, he warned himself as he forced himself to walk past her and into the simple shower area, where he stripped off his clothes with swift angry movements before standing beneath the shower's lukewarm spray.

It took longer than he wanted to acknowledge for the uncomfortably hard, swollen evidence of his arousal to subside; he was still aware of it and Katrina herself when he walked past her without looking at her.

*   *   *

In the darkness of the desert night a horse whinnied shrilly, disturbed by a prowling predator. The sound woke Katrina up.

At first her unfamiliar surroundings confused her, but all too quickly she remembered where she was and why.

Desert nights were bitingly cold, especially in winter, and Katrina shivered as she pulled the still-damp towel around herself before glancing fearfully across the bed.

The empty bed! A small frown puckered her forehead. She looked at her watch. It was three o'clock in the morning and the silken bed cover was smoothly undisturbed. She was alone on the bed, and alone too it seemed in the pavilion's sleeping area.

Surely that wasn't disappointment that she was feeling? Not after all those dreams she had cherished for so long, of the man, her man; her soul mate…the one and only man to whom she would give the whole of herself, with whom she would share the whole of herself. Her first and last lover.

This man, Xander, was not that man! How could he possibly be?

The man she had dreamed of was noble, in spirit and in deed, honourable, good and kind. Xander was none of those things. She could not respect him, nor trust him, and she certainly could not love him, surely?

Maybe not, but she could and did want him! Katrina had to swallow hard against her own feelings. Shock fought with need. Anger with hunger. Caution with urgency, and pride with a wild, fierce passion.

This could not be. She could not…*must* not feel like this.

She slid off the bed, careless of both her nakedness

and the cool air as her mind and her body fought with one another.

What would she really do if he were to come in here now and lay claim to her, to her body? For it was impossible that he would want anything else of her! How would she feel if he were to reach out and touch her, his lean, hard hands shaping her, exploring her, knowing her, cupping her breasts, and then moving lower, over her belly and lower still? A shudder of twisted, dangerous, sensual pleasure ripped through her.

How could she allow herself to think like this? What warped inner part of herself was doing this to her? She had always believed that she would love first and desire second, that it would be a meeting and matching of minds and moral values that would be her prelude to emotional and physical arousal.

There was nothing about Xander or the manner in which he lived his life that remotely equated in any kind of way to her own beliefs or values. He was a liar and maybe a criminal, a man who put his own needs first. How could she possibly want him? The kind of people she admired put others first, and the greater good of mankind.

She needed to breathe fresh air to clear her head. Picking up the towel, she wrapped it firmly around herself and made her way hesitantly through to the outer area of the tent.

Xander had woken up the minute he had heard Katrina move, and when he saw her edging her way to the exit of the tent he pushed back the covers of the impromptu bed that he had made for himself and went after her.

Her hand was on the heavy exit curtain ready to

push it back when Katrina felt Xander's faste...
her bare arm.

'Going somewhere?' he asked her softly.

Immediately she panicked, pulling back from him
and demanding passionately, 'Let go of me.'

Her reaction to him ignited the still-smouldering
embers of Xander's earlier arousal.

Instead of releasing her he tightened his grip on
her, and closed the space between their bodies.

The downward swoop of his head had all the predatory intent of a desert falcon, swift and merciless,
his mouth possessing hers before she could even cry
out in denial.

But it was her own need that was defeating and
betraying her, Katrina acknowledged dizzily as her
mouth clung to his, her lips parting with wanton speed
and eagerness as they offered his probing tongue the
sweet spoils of victory. Longing burned hotly inside
her, melting whatever resistance she might have sum-
moned to her aid as their tongues twined and battled
for the sweetest intimacies of their shared hunger.
Tipping back her head, she let him plunder her mouth,
as she in turn wanted to plunder his. She felt her towel
slipping away from her body, not with a sense of
anxiety, but instead with a wild thrill of female pleasure, for she had already seen—and felt—that the robe
he was wearing hung open over his own nakedness.

If their tongues had meshed savagely together in
mutual eager hunger, that pleasure was just a tame
shadow of how it felt to have him press her the full
length of his body. Her skin, her flesh, her innermost
self was so intensely aroused just by the feel of him
that she pressed herself even closer, moving against
him, craving him as so many centuries ago men had

craved the hashish to which they had become so addicted that it had destroyed them. As the unbearable craving she felt now for Xander would ultimately destroy her?

With a sharp cry of self-disgust she pulled herself away from him and, picking up her towel, fled back to the privacy of the inner chamber.

Would he come after her, and if he did would she be able to be strong enough to deny her body what it was craving? She took a deep breath and held it, nervously fixing her gaze on the curtained doorway, and waited…

But Xander did not appear.

When the breath started to leak painfully from her lungs she told herself that she was glad that he had not come after her.

On the other side of the curtain Xander told himself that Katrina had only pre-empted his own rejection of her by a mere heartbeat. But for the second time in less than twelve hours he had to wait longer than he wanted to admit for the desire for her to slowly and painfully subside to a bearable level.

CHAPTER FOUR

KATRINA frowned in concentration as she sketched the plant she was studying.

She had decided that since she was stuck here at the oasis with no means of escape she might as well put the time to good use, and although he had frowned initially over her request for paper and drawing and writing implements, Xander had produced what she had asked for plus a small stool for her to sit on whilst she worked.

It was three days since she had been kidnapped and nearly three nights since... Quickly she tried to refocus on the plant, but, fascinating though it was, it simply did not have the power to compel her thoughts in the same way that Xander did.

A movement caught her eye and she looked up to see Sulimen standing watching her. A small quiver of apprehension raced down her spine, but determinedly she refused either to acknowledge his presence or to let him see how nervous he was making her feel.

This wasn't the first time she had noticed him watching her, and his presence made her feel on edge and vulnerable.

She tried to continue sketching as though she were completely unfazed by his presence directly in her line of vision, but it was impossible. And impossible too for her not to be aware of the brooding concentration of his gaze as he stared openly and boldly at her.

The way he was looking at her made her wish that she had the protection of the traditional black garments and veils, like those worn by the women she had seen within the camp, to take refuge behind, instead of just her tee shirt and jeans.

But with every second that passed she became more and more on edge and in the end she was forced to concede that her attempts to ignore him were not working, and that the fact that he was continuing to stand boldly staring at her made her feel too uncomfortable to remain.

Turning her back on him, she started to gather up her things, as quickly as she could, telling herself that she would have had to stop working anyway, as the sun was dropping quickly towards the horizon and it would soon be dark.

Seconds later, though, when she headed back towards Xander's tent, Sulimen slipped away into the shadows. Walking through the pitched tents, she was sharply aware of the growing tension that was gripping the whole camp—a combination of a sense of expectancy mingled with something darker and far more dangerous. She gave a small shiver. These were criminals she was living amongst, she reminded herself; men who were outcasts from society because of what they had done. And Xander was one of them, and she had better remember that.

She gave a frightened gasp as she felt a hand on her shoulder, and realised too late that whilst she had been engrossed in her own thoughts Sulimen had emerged from the shadows to catch up with her, and was now subjecting her to a hot-eyed look of sexual greed.

Immediately she pulled away from him, and started

to walk as fast as she could towards Xander's tent, and then broke into a run as her fear overwhelmed her.

'Katrina!'

She came to an abrupt halt as she saw Xander standing in front of her, frowning darkly at her. He wasn't on his own; El Khalid and several other men were with him.

'Tuareg. The woman. How much do you want for her?' she heard Sulimen demanding.

Shock and fear poured through her veins in an icy surge. Sulimen was offering to buy her from Xander? This couldn't be happening. Please, please let it not be happening, she began to panic. But it was.

Wildly she looked into Xander's closed dark face, her mute gaze fixed on him as she prayed that he would not sell her to the other man.

Xander didn't seem disposed to be in any hurry to respond. Was he weighing up how much he could get for her? Or perhaps whether it would be more profitable for him to sell her now to Sulimen rather than to keep her and ransom her once they could return to Zuran City?

She could feel him looking at her. Her pleading, anxious gaze met his; the knowledge that she had to beg him to keep her rubbed her pride raw.

'She is not for sale.'

The terse words made her eyes burn with relieved tears. Without waiting for him to say anything else she almost ran to his side in relief.

But as she quickly discovered, her relief had been premature.

'I will have her,' Sulimen declared angrily. 'I will

give you twice what you can ransom her for, Tuareg. Is that not a fair offer, El Khalid?'

Katrina could see the way El Khalid was looking from Sulimen to Xander.

'The offer is indeed a fair one, Tuareg. I do not wish to have dissent amongst my brothers. It is my wish that you let Sulimen have her.'

Katrina thought she was going to be physically sick, she felt so distraught and afraid.

Sulimen was walking towards them, and she shrank back against Xander's side, making a small sound of acute distress as she did so.

Her vulnerability combined with her fear and his own very real awareness of exactly what kind of man Sulimen was had Xander acknowledging inwardly that he could not in all conscience allow Katrina to be handed over to Sulimen and that he had to do something to protect her. Even without that tell-tale little movement she had made towards him, his own sense of honour and decency would have made it imperative that he did everything he could to prevent such a fate befalling her. But he could think of only one course of action that would save her.

'A thousand apologies, El Khalid, but I cannot do as you ask,' he protested quickly.

'What?'

Katrina could see how infuriated El Khalid looked. His two henchmen were already reaching for the daggers that were stuck into their belts, which, ornate as they were, and as Katrina already had good cause to know, were not in any way merely pretty ornaments.

She couldn't bring herself to look at Xander. She knew that he would have to give her up.

'What is this?' El Khalid was challenging
whilst Sulimen moved closer.

'I have decided to take the woman as my w
Xander announced calmly.

There was a small silence during which Katrina
discovered that she was trembling violently. She
knew that Xander didn't mean it, of course. He was
just claiming that he wanted her as his wife in order
to protect her. As she knew from her study of the
area's history and customs, as a man's intended wife
she immediately became totally off limits to any other
man. Even so...

'He is lying,' Sulimen shouted angrily. 'Do not listen to him!'

Katrina saw El Khalid look from Sulimen's angry,
contorted face to Xander's coolly implacable one.

'I want an end to this matter. We shall soon have
important business to do, and I will not have dissent
amongst my followers. Tuareg, you have said you
want to take the woman as your wife, and so you
shall. You and the woman will both present yourselves to me before my divan tonight. And you,
Sulimen, I do not need to tell you of the penalty for
approaching the wife of another man.'

As he turned to leave El Khalid looked at Xander
and told him, 'You have two hours to prepare yourselves for your wedding.'

They were on their own in the shadows of the tents.
Dusk had fallen but Katrina could see Xander's face
quite plainly in the light of the stars. 'What...
what...did El Khalid mean...about...about our wedding?' she began and then had to stop, as her emotions prevented her from continuing.

'He meant exactly what he said,' Xander informed her coldly. 'We have two hours to prepare ourselves for our marriage.'

'No!' Her denial was instant. Shock and sick disbelief filled her. This couldn't be happening.

'I thought it took weeks to prepare for a wedding in Zuran,' she heard herself protesting shakily. 'And the marriage itself...I thought it went on for several days and...'

'Normally it does, but there is a shorter version, created for circumstances such as these. It isn't so very long ago that different tribes warred with one another and sometimes to marry one's enemy's daughter or sister was a good way of resolving the issue. It has only two requirements, the first being that we present ourselves before El Khalid and declare that we wish to be married. The—'

'But how can we be married?' Katrina demanded numbly.

'Quite easily. By tradition, as the leader of his men El Khalid has the authority to perform such a ceremony. Of course if you would prefer me to hand you over to Sulimen—'

'No,' Katrina stopped him frantically. 'You can't want to marry me.'

'I don't,' he agreed grimly. 'But there is some honour even here amongst thieves and I have heard things of Sulimen that would not allow me to sleep easily with my own conscience were I to let him buy you from me.'

'Buy me! I am a human being and not a...a possession!' she protested wildly.

Immediately Xander took hold of her arm, giving

her a small warning shake as he did so. 'Fine words, but they mean nothing out here.'

'That is barbaric. *You* are barbaric,' she told him, hurling the words at him as her shocked emotions burst through the frail barriers of her self-control.

'This isn't Europe…and it isn't Zuran either,' he answered her. 'The desert is a harsh master and those who inhabit it live by its harsh law—or die.'

There was something about the words he had chosen, the way he was looking at her that sent a curl of icy fear chasing over her nerve endings. Suddenly all the fears and the suspicions she had tried to ignore overwhelmed her.

'What are you all doing out here? What is going on?' she demanded, beginning to panic. 'You are planning something, I know, and I know too that it must be something truly dreadful.' The words were pouring from her in a feverish stream as she finally succumbed to the trauma of everything she had undergone.

'Silence!'

The savage command, accompanied by an even more savage shake, made her tremble from head to foot—with anger and not fear, Katrina decided as she glared furiously at him.

'If you value your life you will not repeat those words!' Xander warned her grimly.

Katrina caught her bottom lip between her teeth as she fought to stop her mouth from trembling. 'If I agree to go through with this…this marriage, I shall want your assurance that it will not be a real marriage!'

'What do you mean by a ''real'' marriage? In the eyes of El Khalid and his followers it will most certainly be real. Or are you asking me if I intend to take you to my bed as tradition says every bridegroom has a right to do with his bride? Even if I did, I wouldn't be able to provide evidence that you came to me with your virtue intact by producing a bloodstained sheet for the tribe's inspection, would I?'

'That was not what I meant!' Katrina could feel her face burning and she was glad of the darkness to conceal her reaction from him.

'I…what I meant… What I wanted was to be assured that the marriage will not be truly legal.'

There was the briefest of pauses before he answered her, but in her anxiety Katrina was unaware of it. 'It will certainly not be legal under European law, or international law,' he told her.

It was the answer she had been hoping for, and she exhaled shakily. She might not want to be forced into this marriage; her pride might rebel in outrage and disgust at Xander's cynical observations and references to her as a possession to be bought and sold, but logically she knew being with him was infinitely preferable to being handed over to Sulimen. But how did she feel emotionally about the situation she was in? That was a question she just did not want to answer. From the first moment she had seen him, her reaction to Xander had been illogical and far too immediate and intense for her to be comfortable with. The harsh flames of reality and everything she had learned about him and his way of life since then should have burnt those foolish tendrils of female longing and desire to ash—she knew that. So why hadn't they? Why couldn't she look at him and see, not a dangerously sensual man whose powerful physical presence affected her like no other man ever had, but a liar and a thief, a man totally devoid of anything in his make-up that could command her respect? Or her love!

A fierce thrill of pain shocked through her. She did not love him! But you want him, an inner voice insisted sharply. You desire him…you ache for him, and if he…

No! No, she was not going to think about this. She was not going to acknowledge it, nor admit to it, and she certainly wasn't going to think about it. She certainly wasn't going to think about the intimacies of marriage to Xander, of being his wife. Of the dark, velvet silence of the desert night and the feel of his hands on her eager body as he reached for her. She wasn't going to think either about the satin heat of his naked body, or the pleasure it would give her to touch his skin, to breathe in its scent, to place her lips against the solid strength of his chest and to… She gave a small violent shudder of rejection and self-disgust. She wasn't going to think about those things because none of them were going to happen!

She could not…would not allow herself to feel this way about a man like Xander. How could she respect herself if she did? How could there be true love without respect? There couldn't!

Grimly Xander stood in the open entrance to his tent and stared unseeingly into the darkness that lay beyond it. He was waiting for Katrina to join him so that they could present themselves before El Khalid and declare their desire to be married to one another. He might have allowed Katrina to believe that their marriage would not be legally binding, but he was well aware that within Zuran such a traditional form of marriage was normally perfectly acceptable and irrevocable. In their case, though, the marriage would have to be formally and legally set aside once his business here was finished. As a member of the ruling family, he needed his half-brother's approval before marrying, and he was confident that his half-brother would be willing to expedite a swift ending of their union. His half-brother would understand that he'd had no option other than to give Katrina the protection of making her his wife. No matter what her lifestyle had been, he could not allow her to be subjected to the fate Sulimen had in store for her. It was no secret around the campfires that amongst his other crimes Sulimen had been accused of both raping and beating at least two women, and that he possessed a streak of sexual carnality and sadism.

None of this, though, was information he could give Katrina.

Earlier in the day he had managed to have a brief secret meeting with the three special agents appointed by the Zuranese Ruling Council who had also infiltrated El Khalid's forces. Like him, they had heard of the important personage with whom El Khalid was expecting to do business, but also like him they had not been able to discover when he would be arriving.

Xander suspected that they were not as fully convinced of the danger to Zuran's ruler as he was himself. He had also heard from his half-brother that Nazir had left Zuran supposedly to deal with his business affairs in Europe.

He heard a small sound behind him and turned round. Katrina was standing hesitantly in the shadows of the tent's living area, her eyes huge and dark with apprehension. His mouth hardened. She was a complication he just did not need!

'A word of warning,' he said grimly as he stepped back inside the tent. 'Once we are married, you cannot do anything that might attract the attentions of other men.'

Katrina glared angrily at him. She had spent the last half an hour wondering how on earth she was going to go through with what lay ahead of her, and trying to fight back her feelings of despair and loneliness. This was not the way she had envisaged herself being married! She ached for the lost protection and love of her patents, for someone of her own she could turn to. But of course there was no one. She was completely alone. Alone and a prisoner, forced into a degrading sham of a marriage for reasons that had nothing whatsoever to do with love.

'How dare you say that to me?' she protested emotionally. 'It's not my fault that Sulimen—'

'No?' The slanting look he was giving her was not a kind one.

'If I had wanted him I would not be here, would I?' she challenged him fiercely.

'I did not say that you wanted him. But maybe you did encourage him? Maybe you were missing the attentions of your lover? Or maybe—'

Katrina curled her fingers into the palms of her hands, her nails digging into her own tender flesh as she seethed with fury. 'I did not encourage him, and Richard was not my lover!'

'That's an easy denial to make, and of course one that cannot be proved!' That was where he was wrong, but Katrina was not going to tell him as much.

As yet no man had been her lover—but of course she was not going to do any such thing!

When she committed herself to a man, and to her love for him and his for her, that commitment would be for ever, and it would involve far more than mere physical intimacy. She had her dreams, even if by some other people's standards they were too idealistic.

'It's time for us to go.'

Xander was holding the curtain aside for her, the tawny gaze fixed on her like a falcon's on its prey.

He was wearing his Tuareg headdress, but instinctively she knew that his mouth would be curved into a hard scimitar-sharp line of disdain and irritation. For all that she had tried to deny it, she was sharply aware that he carried with him a very powerful aura of command and authority. And never more so than tonight.

She had no idea where the richly embroidered over-cloak he was wearing had come from—to judge from its richness it must have once been the property of some very wealthy man. A part of her tried to insist that he should look ridiculous dressed in such theatrical clothes, but another, stronger part of her couldn't help responding to what she could see.

Though she knew he was not, he looked like a man of nobility and power and tradition, a man as forbidding and compelling as the desert itself; a man apart, whose mere presence sent the same shiver of intense reaction whispering over her skin as the awe-inspiring might of this land, which was named so eloquently. He was a man other men would instinctively respect, and whom other women would immediately desire.

As she did?

So much so that she was afraid even to admit to

herself that she was aware of it, never mind accepting the strength of her feelings for him!

Proudly she stood as tall as she could, and looked back at him. 'If you're expecting me to walk mutely several paces behind you—' she began.

'I thought you said you'd studied the history of the desert tribes?' he stopped her immediately.

'I have,' Katrina agreed.

'Well, in that case you should know that Tuareg society is a matriarchal society.'

'But you aren't really Tuareg, are you?' was all she could manage to say as she walked reluctantly to his side.

As they walked a young boy suddenly ran up to Xander's side, and to Katrina's astonishment Xander immediately smiled down at him, putting his hand on the boy's head in a gesture that was almost tender, before saying something to him in a dialect Katrina could not understand.

'He's an orphan,' he explained to her as the boy darted away again. 'I pay him to keep an eye on my horse. The animal is used to company and the boy needs a warm bed.'

Emotions Katrina did not want to feel clogged her throat. For all the harshness he displayed, there was obviously a compassionate, caring side to him.

There was already a distinct chill to the evening air, although whether it was that or her own nervousness that was causing a rash of goose-bumps to break out on her flesh, Katrina didn't want to investigate too thoroughly.

The smell of roasting lamb from the campfires wafted towards them, making her feel slightly sick, her stomach rebelling at the thought of food. By the

time they had reached the clearing where El Khalid
held his nightly meetings, there was a small crowd
waiting to watch the wedding. She could hear music
playing, and women singing.

When she turned apprehensively to look over her
shoulder towards them, Xander told her quietly,
'They will have heard about our marriage and will
have come as is customary to witness it. The music
is a traditional wedding song. There is no need for
you to be afraid.'

He was offering her reassurance? Once again she
had to swallow against an unwanted lump of emotion.

El Khalid was already seated on his makeshift divan, his henchmen surrounding him, the women of
his family grouped behind him along with the musicians.

Katrina froze. She couldn't do it. She couldn't go
through with it. Panic seized her, and she made a
small, inarticulate noise of despair, her gaze darting
frantically around the circle of onlookers surrounding
them as she looked for a way to escape. She was
quivering from head to foot with fear.

'Remember it isn't a real marriage! It doesn't mean
anything!'

The cool, calming words fell against her raw nerve
endings like a soothing balm on burning flesh.

Xander's hand clasped hers, holding it gently, almost as though he was trying to comfort and reassure
her. Wide-eyed, she looked up at him.

The music had stopped. El Khalid was beckoning
them forward. Xander's fingers entwined with her
own. Shakily she started to move forward with him,
not following behind him, but walking at his side.

They had reached the rebel leader. Xander released

her hand and immediately she ached to have him holding it again and for the comfort of that physical contact with him.

Everything that had happened to her was so alien to her, and somehow he had become the only thing that made the brutal nightmare bearable. Without him… Without him she would have been subjected to Sulimen's unchecked demands, without him…

Instinctively she moved closer to him, somehow comforted just by being within the warmth given off by his body, as though it were some kind of magic circle that enfolded and protected her. Just as love was a magic circle that protected and enfolded those who shared it?

Frantically she dragged her thoughts away from such a dangerous road, concentrating instead on El Khalid.

'Give me your hand,' he instructed Katrina.

Reluctantly she did so. Unlike Xander's, his nails were dirty and unkempt, the cuticles bitten and ragged.

'And yours,' he told Xander.

Katrina quivered as Xander placed his lean brown hand over her own and it was clasped and held there by El Khalid.

'Is it the wish of both of you that you should be married?'

Katrina knew the ceremony meant nothing and that it was simply a means to an end, but somehow she discovered that she was affected by it—which was ridiculous. El Khalid was not a man of religion; he was a thief and heaven alone knew what else, and this was just a charade. Nothing more.

'Yes. That is our wish,' she heard Xander saying.

El Khalid was looking at her. Bowing her head, Katrina whispered shakily, 'Yes.'

'Very well, then! As is our custom, it is my right to give this woman to you in marriage, Tuareg.'

Katrina's eyes widened a little with apprehension. El Khalid sounded so solemn.

'Take the woman's hand, Tuareg,' the rebel leader commanded.

Her throat had gone dry and her heart was thudding heavily against her chest wall. Xander was reaching out for her hand, sliding cool, hard fingers between her own, locking her hand to his.

The intimacy of their entwined fingers made her catch her breath, aware of the emotional and sexual significance of their interlocked flesh. Some things needed no words. Palm to palm, flesh to flesh, naked body to naked body, his fingers lying between hers, possessing hers. No wonder an old-fashioned word for marriage was 'hand-fast'.

Her body shuddered and her head seethed with turbulent and frightening thoughts.

El Khalid uttered a sharp command, and a woman, heavily veiled with only her bright dark eyes visible, stepped forward holding a length of silk fabric, so fine that it fluttered in the soft breeze.

Taking it from her, El Khalid started to bind it around both their wrists, muttering some words in Zuranese as he did so. Nervously Katrina risked looking up into Xander's face and then wished she had not done so as she witnessed the grimness of his closed, severe expression.

Her heart was beating slowly and heavily. It felt as though the life force of Xander's blood pulsing through his veins was actually driving her blood through her body as her own pulse matched and echoed the fierce beat of his. The intimate, intense symbolism of what was happening was way, way too much for her to cope with, Katrina recognised emotionally as she felt tears sting the backs of her eyes and her heart lurch against her ribs.

Xander had said that their 'marriage' meant nothing, and maybe it didn't to him, but for her the symbolism of what was happening was a very big 'something' indeed!

Whilst she was still grappling with her feelings, El Khalid spoke some more words over the binding, and then El Khalid turned to Xander and told him, 'You have taken this woman to you as your wife, Tuareg. From now on where you go, she goes. May you be blessed with a long and happy marriage and many children!'

The woman was removing the scarf. Slowly Xander released her hand. Katrina could feel the unsteady, frantic thud of the blood in her veins. The musicians had started to play again. Helplessly she looked into the glinting gold of Xander's eyes. Far from being meaningless, as she had expected, the ceremony had made her feel that they were now joined together in a way that was primitive and eternal. That knowledge filled her with something akin to shocked awe. No matter how many miles might lie between them in the future, nothing ever could or ever would erase what had just happened. How could Xander be so calm about something that to her felt so irreversible?

Logically Katrina knew that other people might think she was overreacting—after all, there was no legal tie between them—but she couldn't help the way she felt about the ceremony they had just undergone. Her hand, her flesh, her very self would bear the imprint of him and their marriage for ever! Shockingly, she felt as though they had shared an intimacy as great as though he had possessed her physically!

The crowd had parted to make a pathway for them. Numbly Katrina let Xander lead her down it whilst the watching men sang and cheered. 'If you're going to faint, at least wait until we get back to the tent,' she heard him say warningly.

CHAPTER FIVE

'WHY didn't you tell me…warn me about…what was going to happen?' Katrina demanded huskily as soon as she knew they could not be overheard.

At her side she felt Xander shrug. 'The binding of our wrists? For the simple reason that I didn't realise that it was going to happen,' he answered her dismissively. 'It's a very old custom, and seldom used any more.'

'Why did they do it that way, then?' she persisted.

'El Khalid's word is law here, not mine,' he pointed out dryly as he started to unwind his head-dress. 'Besides. It was hardly important…'

Xander kept his back to her as he spoke, not wanting her to guess that he too had been strongly affected by the ceremony. By being bound together as they had been, they were now tied to one another in a way that had its roots deep in the tradition of his tribe. He started to frown, not wanting to dwell on the surge of primitive male possessiveness that had filled him.

He could not afford to dwell on such feelings and he certainly could not afford to allow them—or Katrina herself—to become important to him. Immediately he frowned. 'It is a Berber custom, that is all. Don't make too much of it.'

He could see how shocked and distressed she was, and the truth was that he felt equally affected by what had happened himself, but of course he could not afford to let her see that.

'There is no need for us to discuss the subject any further,' he told her, feigning a dismissiveness he was far from feeling, before looking thoughtfully towards the exit. It could well be that Nazir might decide to visit El Khalid tonight, and if he did, then Xander needed to be aware of it.

'I suggest that you retire to the sleeping quarters,' he told Katrina, peremptorily.

Her eyes widened as she listened to him. They hadn't been married more than a handful of minutes and already he was behaving as though she were his to order about as he wished. As though... A hotly dangerous trickle of sensual awareness spread through her. This was her wedding night and if Xander chose...to lay claim to his rights as her husband physically, she would not be able to stop him. The only weapon she had was words.

'This is not a real marriage,' she reminded him. 'You can't tell me what to do.'

'Not as a husband,' he agreed grimly. 'But you appear to be forgetting that I am your captor as well as your husband; you are in my power and you are my possession—to do with as I choose! You will go to the sleeping quarters and you will remain there!'

For what purpose, Katrina wondered feverishly as he stood, arms folded, in front of her, silently waiting for her to obey him.

To be used as though she were a concubine? Her imagination was proving to be her worst enemy, she acknowledged as he turned away from her. But Katrina wasn't ready for their conversation to end.

It was in her nature to want to think the best of everyone, she tried to reassure herself. And that was the reason she wanted Xander to prove to her that he had some redeeming qualities. For his sake or for her own? Because of her inability to deny the attraction she felt towards him, the desire she felt for him? She must not allow such thoughts to take root, she warned herself. And besides, any attraction she might think she felt for Xander now would soon disappear once she was free and living her normal life. Even so, somehow she could not prevent herself from asking him.

'Why did you marry me? Was it because of the ransom money you hope to get for me or was it really because you wanted to protect me? To save me from Sulimen?'

She saw the liquid flash of his darkly intent gaze as he turned his head to look at her. She felt as though it were burning into her, seeking out all those things she most wanted to keep secret. For a man who earned his living in such a shameful manner he possessed a proud arrogance that should have been risible, but which instead suited him perfectly, she acknowledged unwillingly.

It was very, very rare for anything or anyone to catch him off guard, but Katrina had done exactly that, Xander admitted grimly. It was almost as though she was actually looking for a reason to think better of him, he recognised incredulously.

An austere look darkened his face. Had she somehow seen through his camouflage and the subterfuge he had been forced to adopt, to the person he really was? Could she sense his vulnerability where she was concerned? Could she feel it in the tense air between them? The hard heat of his desire for her, and the struggle he was having in fighting against it? The fierce longing he felt to take her in his arms and make the vows they had just exchanged a reality?

He had actually taken steps towards her before he managed to remind himself of the real situation. She was a modern young woman who was no doubt used to using her sexuality to get what she wanted, if she chose to do so.

'What are you hoping I will say? That I married you to save you? Are you hoping that I might be vulnerable to you myself and that you could use that against me in some way? Perhaps seduce me into giving you your freedom?' he taunted her silkily, whilst Katrina's face burned a dark, hot red.

'I might have known you would think something like that!' she retorted bitterly. 'That Machiavellian mind of yours wouldn't allow you to think anything else, would it?'

'What else is there to think?' Xander retaliated grimly.

'For your information, I was hoping that I might have found something in you that I could respect!' Katrina told him shakily. 'Some saving grace that would mean—'

'That you could manipulate me at will,' Xander stopped her curtly.

She was touching a place in his emotions he didn't want to have touched by anyone, but least of all by her. Her words came far too close to his own private thoughts on the subject of love and marriage. According to his half-brother, his mother and father had loved one another very deeply. Certainly enough for them both to step outside the familiar boundaries of their own cultures in order to be together. Such a love cast a very long shadow and he knew that he wanted a union as strong as that. But his pride was fiercely strong. He could never, ever love a woman he did not respect. And growing up in his father's culture had ensured that he could not respect a woman who was sexually or indeed emotionally promiscuous.

For any woman, but even more a woman such as Katrina, to dare to accuse him of not being worthy of her respect irked and infuriated him. For such an insult she would have to be punished!

'I'm not your foolish, weak, easy-to-seduce English lover,' he said contemptuously. 'He might be easily bedazzled by the fake glitter of the tawdry goods you have on sale and unable to see that they and you have no true worth, but I am not so easily pleased or deceived.'

Katrina's mouth had gone very dry. Her whole body was feeling the impact of the insult he had just delivered and its thinly veiled implications regarding her sexual morals.

'You have no right to say such things to me,' was all she could manage to say as she somehow managed to choke out the words above the brittle fragility of her emotional defences.

He knew how to hurt, and how to wound and maim. Katrina couldn't imagine that any woman would want to be forced to listen to a man speaking about her in such a way.

'And in case you've forgotten, Richard was not my lover!' she told him fiercely.

Xander gave a dismissive shrug. 'I have no interest in who has or has not shared your bed and your favours.'

He was lying and he knew it, but what else could

he do? He had to finish this conversation and find out if Nazir had arrived, for his half-brother's sake.

'I have to go out,' he announced tersely. 'And don't wait for me so that you can try and persuade me again. My advice to you is not to bother wasting your time.'

He gave her a look that stripped her pride to the bone and left it and her mercilessly exposed.

There were so many angry words she wanted to hurl at him, but it was already too late. His hand was already lifting the heavy curtain, and he was stepping through it, leaving her alone to confront the unpalatable reality behind her angry reaction to their conversation.

No matter how hard she fought to ignore it, the word 'seduce' hung dangerously in her thoughts. He might have been wrong about there being any intention on her part to seduce him, but that word on his lips had caused her stomach to clench and her heart to flip over whilst her legs had turned weak and the slow ache of longing pulsing deep inside her had flared into a hungry, driving beat.

No, she did not want to seduce him, but shamingly she acknowledged that she could not say the same in reverse. What on earth was the matter with her? He was a criminal, callous, arrogant and dishonest. There was not one single redeeming thing about him. And she was a fool for trying to find something in him she could respect, some excuse for him she could use to justify her feelings for him.

It was not even as though he had done or said anything to make her think he shared her confusing and disturbing feelings in any kind of way—quite the opposite. Her whole body burned with indignation as she remembered the contemptuous way in which he had spoken to her. He was not just unprincipled and untrustworthy, he was bigoted as well! It would have given her a great deal of pleasure to have thrown his words back at him and told him that she had not in fact had any lovers, never mind the scores he had chosen to imply, but of course that was something she could and would not do. Her virginity was a life-style choice she had made because of her own profound and private beliefs and not so that she could demean herself by claiming it in front of someone like Xander.

He simply wasn't worthy of the foolish feelings she was silly enough to have for him, and for her own sake she had to root them out of her heart immediately. If only it were that easy. She gave a small shiver. There was something dark and dangerous about him, something raw and untamed that the female core of her responded to wantonly and rebelliously, and there was nothing she could do about it, she admitted despairingly.

As he made his way silently through the camp, his movements as fluid and as soft-footed as a mountain lion, Xander derided himself grimly for the fierce surge of male hunger Katrina had made him feel. His mind might question how he could possibly want such a woman, but his body was questioning even more fiercely how he could resist her.

She affected him as no other woman had ever done, in a thousand and one different ways, every single one of which was unwelcome. There was no place in his life for this kind of situation and no place in his pride for the kind of need she aroused in him.

As he neared El Khalid's tent he forced himself to put Katrina out of his mind and to focus instead on his half-cousin Nazir, and the reason he himself was here. He'd been wondering whether he'd made a dangerous error of judgement. The special agents were doubtful about Nazir's involvement. But Nazir was planning to strike against the Ruler, Xander was convinced of that. It was just a question of how and when.

He had reached El Khalid's tent, and he kept himself concealed in the shadows. A small frown creased his forehead beneath his disguise as he heard the sound of a moving vehicle. A smart four-wheel-drive vehicle swept in from the desert, creating its own personal sandstorm, the vehicle skidding to a sharp halt within a short walk from the rebel leader's group of tents. Xander could hardly believe his own luck as he watched the doors open and two heavily armed guards get out, quickly followed by his half-cousin.

Before they could reach El Khalid's tent the rebel leader himself emerged from it, coming forward to greet Nazir, bowing low in front of him before inviting him into the tent.

So he'd been right after all! This was something the special agents needed to know about, Xander acknowledged, and now! Quietly he began to make his way to their tent.

CHAPTER SIX

KATRINA woke abruptly from the wantonly erotic and symbolic dream she'd been having, in which she had been carried in the folds of a richly hued carpet into the tent of a powerful warrior who'd borne a heart-shaking resemblance to Xander—in the same way that Cleopatra had offered herself to Anthony.

Her face burned as she tried to ignore the sensuality of her dream and the manner in which she had presented herself to Xander, her body clad in diaphanous rainbow-coloured veils so sheer that her body had been openly visible through them. Her nipples had been painted with a soft gold paste, her sex lightly covered in a sheath of the transparent silk that had done far more to enhance its mystery than modestly protect it.

As she had advanced towards Xander her kohl-painted eyes had seen how he had tried not to show any interest in her, and her pink-stained mouth had parted on a small female breath of wanton knowingness when her gaze had slid from his face to his manhood, which had been openly straining against the cloth that had constrained it as his body had given her female power that his facial expression would not.

Her tongue had pressed against her parted lips whilst she had boldly moved closer to him, her whole body heavy with sweet, hot desire for him, and ready for the promise held by the swollen flesh of his manhood.

Not one single word had he spoken to her as she'd reached the raised dais on which he'd been seated, but she had witnessed his swiftly indrawn breath as she'd mounted it without asking his permission. She'd walked proudly towards him instead of humbly awaiting his permission to draw closer to him.

Only once she had reached him had she dropped gracefully to her knees in front of him, the high, taut thrust of her gilded breasts swelling eagerly beneath his hooded gaze as they'd flaunted their eager desire for his touch.

Slowly and deliberately she had reached out towards him, placing her fingertips on his thigh, only a breath away from the thick outline of his penis. When she had exhaled in heady excitement and arousal, she had felt the outer lips of her own sex swell and the small secret place of pleasure within them throb eagerly.

She had lifted her hand to close it over his hardness, but before she had been able to do so he had reached for her, dragging her onto his lap, and holding her there whilst his mouth had fastened fiercely on one gilt-tipped nipple, his tongue tip playing with its quivering hardness whilst his hand had opened her thighs, and pushed away the shimmering veils of silk, so that the eager wetness of her sex had been fully open to his touch.

Her small cry of wanton pleasure had elicited from him an immediate response of triumphant reaction.

Long, deft fingers had parted the enclosing folds of flesh, and when her body had jerked against his touch in mute, hot, sensual delight, his mouth had tugged fiercely on her sensitised nipple so that she had been burning with aching need for him.

His fingers had moved more intimately on her, first one and then another erotically rubbing against the wetness and then probing the innermost heart of her. When she had cried out to him in sweet, hot, eager need, he had spread her thighs wider and taken her mouth in a savagely passionate kiss that had stolen her breath, and with it her reason. The stroking caress of his fingertip against the small, secret nub of flesh that had swelled for his touch had caused her whole body to tighten on the edge of shockingly intense pleasure. She had felt the waves of it radiating out and she had lifted her body against it, wanting more of it, and of him!

She didn't want to remember any more, especially not the very real sensation of being poised on the edge of her own orgasm. Shamefully she still ached with the physical arousal her dream had caused, Katrina recognised, mortified that she should have had such a dream at all, never mind about Xander. She was grateful for her solitude and for the darkness that hid the hot burn of her face. And the hot burn of her body?

She lay rigidly still in the darkness almost afraid to let herself go back to sleep.

In another three hours or so it would be dawn. Xander stood completely still in the silence of the tent. The special agents had agreed that as soon as El Khalid had announced the purpose of Nazir's visit to the men he had gathered around him, they would leave the camp and report their findings to the Ruling Council.

Xander's mouth compressed. He had urged them not to delay, but they had remained adamant. They were not prepared to recommend a move against

Nazir until they had unassailable proof that he meant to harm Zuran's Ruler.

From inside the sleeping area of the tent he could hear the soft little sound Katrina made in her sleep. Katrina... His wife... But another man's woman? Probably more than just one other man's woman! A primitive, all-male feeling of mingled anger and jealousy ripped through him. He took a step towards the sleeping area, and then froze. What he was feeling was merely a shimmering mirage, he told himself fiercely. It had no reality to it, and if he ignored it and refused to acknowledge it or give it room in his heart or head then it would disappear. And so too would the urgent, hungry stirring of his body.

Katrina woke up briefly and muzzily at the sound of the morning calls to prayer, but the events of the previous day had taken their toll, and sleep was claiming her again before she could stop it.

Xander on the other hand was already awake, tension coiling his body like a tightly wound spring. As soon as the call to morning prayers had died away, news swept through the camp, like dust carried on the desert wind, that El Khalid had had an important visitor. An immediate meeting had been called to discuss his visit with his men.

Like the other men, Xander made his way to the open area in front of El Khalid's tent, taking care to position himself close to the three disguised special agents, but not directly with them. He was pretty sure that at least two of the men now stationed outside El Khalid's tent were in reality Nazir's personal guards and he suspected they would have been instructed to report back to their master if they saw anything they considered suspicious or not in Nazir's best interests.

El Khalid's speech to them was brief and to the point. He and his men were being hired to infiltrate the National Day celebrations in Zuran and cause civil unrest.

'No mention was made of any attempt to harm your brother,' one of the agents pointed out sharply to Xander when the meeting was over.

'Nazir will not entrust anyone else to assassinate my brother. He will kill him himself under cover of the rioting El Khalid will cause. Officially he will be out of the country, we already know this. There is no doubt in my mind that this is what he plans to do,' Xander told the agents grimly. 'My guess is that he will disguise himself as one of El Khalid's men, and strike when my brother makes his traditional walk amongst his people.'

'We have no proof that this is what he plans to do,' one of the agents objected.

'Are you prepared to take the risk that I am wrong?' Xander challenged him. 'The life of the Ruler is more important.'

There was a small silence and then another member of the trio said firmly, 'We are leaving now to make our report. As soon as we are out of radio range from the camp we shall phone for a helicopter to pick us up. Our report will be delivered to the Ruling Council within a matter of hours. We shall recommend that an armed force be dispatched here to this camp immediately to surround it and take everyone here into custody. If you are correct then that will surely include Nazir.'

Xander knew that this was as much as he could

hope for, and that it was as pointless chivvying the agents as it was to beg his half-brother to think of his own safety and to cancel his traditional public walk-about on Zuran's National Day.

The sun was warming the desert as he strode back through the camp, the smell of cooking food filling the air.

It was the scent of freshly brewing coffee that woke Katrina from her heavy sleep. For a few precious seconds between waking and remembering she basked lazily in the comfort of her bed and the delicious coffee smell, and then abruptly reality returned with menacing darkness.

She was not just a prisoner; she was also now married to her captor! She looked down at her wrist. She was bound now to Xander. She sat up in the bed, feeling slightly sick and dizzy.

As always she listened edgily for any sounds that would indicate where Xander was before sliding out of the bed and hurrying into the small bathroom. Once there she showered quickly, her face suddenly suffused with hot colour as she felt the unfamiliar sensitivity of her breasts when she soaped her skin. Last night might only have been a dream but it had still left as much of an actual physical memory with her body as if Xander had really made love to her.

It was a relief to dry herself and pull on her clothes so that she no longer had to see the openly eager, swollen thrust of her own nipples.

Two minutes later she was standing beside the curtain that separated the areas of the tent from one another. Taking a deep breath, she exhaled slowly whilst reminding herself of just what Xander was. He was not the man her vulnerable heart longed for him to be. Far from it. That man was simply a creation of her own foolish emotions.

Determinedly she pulled back the curtain and stepped into the outer area. Xander was standing several feet away watching her. A bloom of delicate pink colour washed tellingly over her face as she battled to meet his gaze and failed.

This man was her husband; she was joined to him now and that joining was surely in its own way just as intimate as if he had taken her in his arms last night and to his bed. A tremor like that of a young gazelle shivered through her.

Watching her, Xander acknowledged grimly that the blush staining her skin and her modestly downcast look were everything that an old-fashioned husband might expect from a new bride on the first morning of her marriage. And no doubt had they been such a couple, having witnessed her self-conscious modesty he would have gone immediately to her and swept her into his arms, taking her back to the bed they had so recently shared to show her fresh delights and pleasures.

But of course they were no such thing.

Whilst he removed the long scarf of indigo-coloured cloth that acted both as his means of disguise and proclaimed him as Tuareg, a bitter, almost cruel smile hardened his mouth. Katrina was as far removed from an innocent shy bride as it was possible to get. How many other lovers had there been before the cowardly fool who had abandoned her in order to save himself? He could feel his ancestry and upbringing battling against the European blood of his mother.

How could he ever hope to find a woman who

could both accept and understand both opposing sides of him, and at the same time appeal to both of them in a way that made him feel he needed and loved her so much that he could not bear to live without her?

How indeed! He already knew that he could not. And right now he was more than happy to live his life without a woman. After all he had far more important things to worry about.

'There was a lot of noise and excitement a little while ago,' Katrina announced, bravely trying to act as though everything was normal, and not in any way as though she was acutely conscious of the fact that last night they had been married and she was now in the eyes of those who had witnessed that marriage Xander's wife, but also his possession!

'No more than normal,' Xander lied coolly, before adding tauntingly, 'What were you hoping? That your lover had come to rescue you?'

Angry colour flamed up under her skin. 'I was simply trying to make conversation,' she informed him sharply.

'I've brought you this,' Xander said, ignoring both her comment and her anger as he produced one of the all-enveloping black garments worn by women in public.

'In future you will not leave the tent unless you are wearing it.'

Katrina's eyes rounded both with shock and disbelief.

'I will do no such thing!' she refused immediately.

'You will not leave this tent unless you are wearing the robes,' Xander repeated before adding ominously, 'And if you do not agree to do so, then you will leave me with no choice other than to take steps to ensure your compliance.'

'By doing what?' Katrina challenged him fiercely. 'By dressing me in it yourself?'

'No,' he answered her evenly. 'If you do not agree, then I shall simply make sure that you are not able to leave the tent. If necessary by tethering you inside it in the same way that a goat herder might fetter his goats.'

Katrina could hardly believe her ears as she recoiled from the primitiveness of his threat.

She couldn't trust herself to speak, so instead she let her body language voice her outrage and fury to him as she looked coldly past him.

'It is time for us to eat. Pick it up and put it on,' Xander ordered her calmly.

'I will not wear it,' she told him stubbornly. 'It smells of another woman's perfume,' she added angrily.

Xander made no response. He'd had to haggle hard and pay way over what it was worth in order to persuade one of El Khalid's women to part with the garment. His own keen nose acknowledged that the heaviness of the other woman's perfume did cling to the fabric, but he had to make sure that Katrina took his threat seriously—for her own sake as much as anything else. If Nazir was going to return to the camp as Xander suspected he would, then he did not want his half-cousin to see Katrina and wonder suspiciously what a European woman was doing here. If he thought that Katrina posed the slightest degree of risk to him, Nazir would kill her, without any qualms whatsoever. Xander had no doubt about that, and so for her own sake she had to be protected. As the wife of a Tuareg tribesman wearing the robes she would not arouse Nazir's suspicions in the way a European woman would.

'You must wear it for your own safety,' he told her quietly.

The unexpectedness of something that could almost have been genuine concern for her in his voice caught and held Katrina's attention. Was there a warmer, caring side to his nature after all?

'Because of Sulimen?' she guessed, unable to hide her fear.

Immediately Xander took a step towards her, as though he wanted to reassure her. 'Have no fear, he shall not harm you. I shall see to that, but it will be expected by the women that you will dress as they do and by the men that you dress as my wife. Truly it is for your own protection that you must dress traditionally.'

Instinctively she knew that he was speaking the truth. Yet again, she could feel herself reacting to his compassion. And to him! More to give herself something to do than for any other reason, she picked up the black garment and pulled it on, grimacing a little as she did so, unable to stop herself from wrinkling her nose against its strong scent.

Quickly Xander shielded his eyes from her, not wanting her to read in his expression how relieved he was not to be tormented by the subtle natural scent of her own body and the far too powerful and dangerous effect it had on him whenever he was close enough to her to breathe it in.

It took Katrina several minutes to settle the all-encompassing folds of the robes—made quite obviously for someone much larger than she was herself—

comfortably around her own slender person. During which time, Xander strode past her and into the bedroom, emerging almost immediately carrying a sheet.

Uncomprehendingly Katrina watched as he unfolded it, and then deliberately squeezed it in his powerful hands to crumple it a little before unsheathing his dagger, pushing up the sleeve of his robe and making a small cut on the inside of his arm, which immediately began to bleed.

Balling up the centre of the sheet, he held it against the cut.

'What are you doing?' she asked him in bewilderment.

'As El Khalid's mother reminded me when I bartered with her cousin for the robe, it is a tribal custom amongst the nomad population that a blood-stained sheet is produced on the morning after a young woman is married as proof of her virginity. Your failure to be declared a virgin bride will dishonour both you as my wife and me as your husband.'

Katrina was outraged beyond words and could only stare at him in white-faced revulsion.

After what Xander had just told her, the last thing she felt able to do was to show herself in public!

'What is it?' Xander demanded as she stepped back from him and started to remove her enfolding black robes.

'I've decided that I'm not hungry,' she told him woodenly.

The look he was giving her smashed through her fragile self-control and before she could stop herself she was demanding emotionally, 'Do you really think I am going to let you parade me along with that sheet to satisfy other people's prurient curiosity?'

She could hear the threat of tears in her own voice and tried to fight them away, gulping in air as she did so. She would not, could not cry in front of him. How could she have thought him compassionate?

'You must not judge us as though we were Europeans. We are not. There is nothing prurient in this traditional act. Far from it. And it is designed to protect your sex, not to humiliate it.'

'How do you work that one out?' Katrina challenged him bitterly.

'Easily,' Xander told her coolly. 'For instance, the nomad tribes lived dangerous lives. Men fought and were often killed. If a man died, his family could refuse to accept his wife's child unless they had proof that she'd been a virgin when they'd married. Proof of a bride's virginity protects her honour, and the honour of her family. A Tuareg girl in your position would accompany her husband proudly to this showing of the proof of her virgin state.'

'Maybe, but I am not a Tuareg woman,' Katrina told him fiercely.

'You are not a virgin either,' Xander said coldly.

'Yes, I—' Katrina began heatedly.

She was silenced as Xander cut across her with a sharply curt, 'I am hungry even if you are not.' He started to rewind the covering Tuareg cloth around his head and lower face. He looked austere and compelling and her stupid heart was turning over as though it actually enjoyed the aura of subtle magnificence and danger he gave off. Pausing only to gather up the sheet, he cast her a brief hard look and headed for the exit.

She could not follow him. She just could not, Katrina admitted as she watched him leave.

CHAPTER SEVEN

HALF an hour later Katrina's stomach was growling hungrily, but she ignored the noise it was making.

'I've brought you some coffee and some food.'

Katrina whirled round and stared as Xander stepped back into the tent carrying a pot of coffee and a small dish piled high with fruit and small cakes. He had brought her some food? Confusion darkened her eyes. She had mentally labelled him as cruel and sadistic, but right now he was behaving with a thoughtfulness and concern that was proving her wrong. And not for the first time! These glimpses of another side of him both tormented and delighted her. It was as though somewhere deep inside her a small spring of happiness had welled up and was bubbling over.

'Luckily for you El Khalid's mother has decided that your refusal to show yourself this morning is a sign of your modesty.'

But he did not think she was modest! Her joyful happiness was extinguished by angry pain.

Xander was placing the coffee pot and the dish down on a low table and, despite the intensity of her feelings, Katrina realised how hungry she was.

'I have to go out—remember you are not to leave this tent unless you are properly robed and veiled.'

Katrina waited until he had gone before pouncing on the food. The coffee smelled heavenly and tasted even better, the fruit sharp and juicy on her taste buds, whilst the small, sweet almond pastries melted on her tongue.

As he busied himself checking on his horse Xander's mind was in reality far from totally focusing on the patient animal that was nuzzling his shoulder so affectionately.

Why had he allowed the thought of Katrina with another man to affect him so intensely? Why had he allowed himself to be so aroused by the sight of her that he had had to leave the tent in order to put a safe distance between them? Surely he was not fool enough to be affected by a centuries-old marriage ritual, was he? It had after all been nothing more than a necessity, the only way he'd had of protecting Katrina from Sulimen, and he had already made up his mind to ask his half-brother to have the marriage set aside.

Xander rubbed gently behind the mare's ears. She was pure Arab bloodstock and bred from one of his half-brother's prized stallions. Her wise dark eyes reflected her breeding and her purity.

Why had he allowed himself to be so affected by the dark smudges beneath Katrina's eyes this morning? Why had he wanted to go to her and kiss the soft tremble from her mouth? Such thoughts, such feelings were virtually akin to insanity. There was no place for them in his life.

Having checked on the mare, he walked as casually as he could in the direction of the oasis, sauntering easily as though merely passing the time. Whilst El Khalid might have cautioned his most trustworthy men to keep a watch on the rest of them, Nazir most undoubtedly would have left his own loyal spies behind to ensure his own safety.

Xander was tempted to telephone his half-brother. His mobile was in his pocket, but he was concerned that Nazir might be intercepting the Ruler's telephone calls, even though officially he was supposed to be out of the country.

Xander frowned as a small sound caught his attention. Shading his eyes, he stared towards the horizon, watching the small dot that was a low-flying helicopter grow larger.

Nazir! It had to be! And what better means of re-entering Zuran and then leaving the city quickly once he had achieved his goal and murdered the Ruler? Had Nazir told El Khalid what he intended to do? Somehow Xander doubted it. Not that the rebel leader would shrink from the violence of murder. No, he would not do that but he would certainly demand a great deal of money to be involved in it!

And besides Nazir was far too wily to give anyone the kind of information that could ever be used against him. No. The Ruler's death would publicly be attributed to the rebels, Xander acknowledged.

The helicopter, camouflage painted and without any identifying markings, was coming closer. Xander turned his back on it and pretended to be studying the oasis. There was no sense in drawing attention to himself by appearing to be too curious.

He wanted to be there, though, when the helicopter landed, so he started to make his way back to the camp.

As was only to be expected, the arrival of the helicopter was causing a flurry of curiosity and speculation, and Xander attached himself to the group of men standing closest to it.

A man was climbing out of the stationary aircraft

and, although he had disguised himself by growing a beard, and wearing traditional robes instead of the Western-style Italian suits he normally favoured, Xander had no trouble whatsoever in recognising his half-cousin simply from the way he moved.

So he had been right! Good as it felt to have his suspicions of Nazir confirmed, Xander's overriding emotion was one of anger against Nazir. He had received nothing but love and generosity from the Ruler, but his greed and lust for power were such that he was ready to murder him in order to step into his shoes. No way was Xander going to allow that to happen! He did feel happier now, though, knowing that he would be able to keep Nazir under closer observation.

El Khalid had come out of his tent to greet the new arrival, bowing low before him as he made him welcome. As casually as he could, Xander moved closer, trying to overhear what the two men were saying to one another.

It was over an hour since Xander had left, and Katrina had grown bored with sitting cooped up in the tent.

Defiantly she got up and walked determinedly towards the exit. There was no reason why she should allow him to tell her what to do. She wasn't really his wife, after all.

The thought of Xander, treating her as an equal, respecting her, loving her, was causing a surge of complex emotions within her that she knew she was not currently strong enough emotionally to handle.

And whilst she might not really be Xander's wife, she was his prisoner, she reminded herself.

How much was he planning to demand for her return? The government department for whom she worked was a small one, with very limited funds. Or was he thinking that she would have family who would be prepared to pay him for her release? One heard of such things, hostages being taken and then ransomed, but she had never envisaged such a fate befalling her!

She wished that she could be brave enough to try to escape, but the camp was heavily guarded. Even if she could evade those guards, she knew what would happen to her if she succeeded in getting away from the oasis. She would die in the desert.

Of course she could try to steal a vehicle, but it would have to be one with a modern satellite navigation system installed in it, she admitted wryly, plus a full tank of petrol.

It made much more sense to remain where she was.

Sense? That was what was motivating her, was it? Was she really sure about that? Was she totally sure that she was not being influenced by those dangerous emotions she knew she felt for Xander, and that she was not secretly longing for…? For what? she challenged herself angrily. Her face had grown hot. She could feel the now familiar and distinctive intimate ache seizing her body.

This was the twenty-first century; women no longer needed to hide the fact that they could experience physical desire as a need in itself and by itself. They no longer had to tell themselves that physical desire could only be born out of love. They had every right if they wished to do so to engage in physical intimacy without any emotional commitment, for the simple reason that it pleased them to do so. To be blunt about it, if they so desired, they could have sex with a man and then walk away from him. Could she do that? Did she really want to?

As she paced the carpeted floor of the tent, her mind on her own deep thoughts and not on what was underfoot, she stubbed her toe on the edge of a wooden box just protruding from beneath the low divan.

Frowning, she bent to rub her toe, and then kneeled down intending to push the box out of the way, but instead she discovered that she was actually tugging it out of its place of semi-concealment, panting a little as she did so because of its weight.

What was inside it? She had no right to look, she told herself, but despite that she still lifted the lid.

Inside the chest were several books. No wonder it had been heavy. Carefully she lifted the top one out, her breath catching on a small gasp as she did so. These weren't just books, they were works of art, books fit for the library of a connoisseur—a very wealthy connoisseur, leather-bound, and tooled, with thick gold lettering on the spine, the pages goldedged. When it had been new, such a book would have been very expensive. Reverently Katrina opened it. A first edition. A collector's item, and probably extremely rare. It was a book of poetry, including amongst others Robert Browning's poems for Elizabeth Barrett. Inscribed inside it in elegant handwriting were the words:

'For my own beloved Elizabeth.'

Hot, emotional tears misted her eyes. Such simple words, but to her they were of more value than a thousand first editions. This book had been a gift of love; it had been given with love. Very gently she closed it, and put it down before removing another from the box.

This one was French—the belles-lettres of an author whose name she did not recognise, but like its fellow it was dedicated to 'Elizabeth'. And the strong male signature on it was set above the familiar crest of the Ruler of Zuran.

Her heart skipped a beat. That must surely mean that the books had come originally from the royal palace. And that Elizabeth, whoever she was, had been deeply loved by a royal prince.

She picked out another one—this time a book written in Arabic.

She didn't need to be an expert to guess that these books were worth a fortune and irreplaceable, Katrina acknowledged, but of far more value and importance in her eyes was not their material worth but the sentimental value demonstrated by the inscriptions. Those books had been a gift of love, to a woman very deeply loved.

Everything about them said that they had been cherished and treasured, but now they were in Xander's possession, and she was in no doubt as to how they had got there. They had been stolen from their rightful owner, Katrina acknowledged bleakly.

Although she wasn't cold, she shivered. Why was she feeling so shocked? She had already known what Xander was, hadn't she?

That incident in the alleyway, his cold-hearted avowal to ransom her; discovering that he possessed stolen goods should not be causing her the sick misery that it was. Slowly, her heart aching, she started to replace them in the box, pausing with the last one.

'What do you think you are doing?'

She hadn't heard Xander come in, and she jumped in shock, almost dropping the book as she heard the savage fury in his voice. She wasn't going to give into it, though—nor to him. Scrambling to her feet, she turned to confront him, but he was ignoring her, kneeling instead to examine the contents of the chest, before closing the lid and removing a small key from his belt, which he used to lock it.

'How dare you pry amongst my possessions?' he said savagely.

'Your possessions!' Katrina challenged him bravely. 'Those books do not belong to you. I saw the inscription. You stole them from someone!'

Xander could hardly believe what he was hearing. Katrina had been rifling through his personal possessions—the treasured mementoes he had of his parents—and she had the gall to accuse him of stealing them! In the intensity of his fury, Xander forgot all the reasons Katrina believed she had to question his honesty, and remembered only how protectively he had always cherished the books that had been his father's love gift to his mother before their marriage.

That feeling had meant so much to him as a small child, unable to articulate his feelings properly, only knowing that holding the books somehow made him feel as though he was clinging to a part of the mother he had never known. They had become his talisman and he never went anywhere without them. Were any of El Khalid's rebels to find them he would of course have to pretend he had stolen them, but it was an unwritten law amongst the rebels that they respected one another's privacy and possessions.

A law that was not observed by Katrina, though! And now here she was, the woman who had already caused him more sleepless nights and disturbed thoughts than she had any right to do, daring to claim that he had no right to his mother's possessions.

'The books are mine,' he told her fiercely, obvious anger darkening his eyes.

Katrina was in no mood to believe him, though. She gave him a look of contemptuous disbelief. 'That's impossible. They are worth a fortune—museum pieces, first editions,' she pointed out sharply.

Xander was standing up now, and far too close to her, towering over her, filling the air around her with his hostility. Too late she recognised exactly what effect her words were having on him and how furiously and dangerously angry he was. A small pulse was beating heavily in the hollow of his throat, and fury blazed from his eyes. Apprehensively she tried to move away, and started to step back from him, but her action simply brought her up against the hard edge of the divan.

'Do you actually dare to accuse me of being a liar?' he demanded with soft savagery as he stepped closer to her—so soft that the cold words were little more than the icy chill of breath against her skin.

Katrina was not going to allow herself to give in to him! Why should she?

'You are a liar!' she threw back at him recklessly. 'A liar and a thief!'

The fierily passionate words, the contempt he could hear in her voice and see in her eyes burnt Xander's pride as though it had been acid.

Katrina winced as he took hold of her upper arms, gripping them so tightly that it hurt.

'You will not say such things to me, do you hear me?' he thundered furiously.

'Why not? I am only speaking the truth!' Katrina retaliated, her own fury as great as his.

'Those books were a gift to me from my mother.' Xander couldn't hold back the words any longer. They felt as though they had been torn physically from his heart, and had left behind a place that burned with bitter pain.

Katrina stared at him, unable to credit what she was hearing. Did he really expect her to believe him?

She could almost taste the intensity of their emotions in the air surrounding them, bitter as aloes and sharp on her tongue.

She could feel the heat coming off Xander's body, and shockingly she could feel too her own immediate and undeniable female response to it—and to him. Panic twisted through her outrage. How could she feel like this? How could she be remotely aroused by a man she could not respect? She must not feel like this. She was having to fight to hold onto reality.

'That isn't possible.' She forced herself to make the denial, praying that he wouldn't see in her eyes how intensely she wished that it were and that he were not just telling her the truth, but also that he were finally admitting her into his confidence and allowing her to learn something about his true background.

But of course he was not! And knowing that was hurting her far, far more than she was able to cope with. She had to fight against the pain of her own emotions to make herself tell him quietly, 'The books bear the signature of the Ruler of Zuran.'

The words seemed to drop into the tense silence as heavily as stones in deep, still water. She couldn't bear to look at him. She couldn't bear to see in his eyes that he knew she could not be deceived. The tension in the room was such that it felt like an invisible pressure all around her, crushing her. She had to struggle to expand her lungs enough to draw in air.

'There's no point in continuing to lie to me, Xander,' she told him huskily. 'I can't believe you. You are a liar and a—'

The despairing resignation in her voice sliced into Xander's pride, and worse, he realised on a sharp, spearing pain of shock, her refusal to believe him was piercing him with searing emotional pain, like nothing he had previously experienced and which he just could not endure.

'Enough!' He groaned out the word as though he were dying, reaching for her, to silence both her and his own pain in the only way he could, with the hard pressure of his mouth on hers.

It was a kiss given in anger and in punishment, a deliberate branding of male domination, but the moment he felt her mouth beneath his something happened inside him that Xander knew he could neither resist nor control. Some alchemy over which he had no power transformed his anger into hunger, her punishment into his own as his senses ached with longing, overturning all the barriers he had so carefully erected against his own vulnerability towards her.

The softness of her mouth, the slight quiver of her body, the sweetness of her taste as his tongue drove possessively between her parted lips, sent desire leaping along his nerve endings, to every cell of his body.

He wanted her more than he had ever wanted anyone or anything... He wanted her...to taste her, hold her, possess her, lay his own mark upon her for the whole of eternity.

Thoughts, feelings…needs ran through him like quicksilver, and he was powerless to stop them, powerless to do anything other than respond to the driving need that possessed him. The driving need for him to possess her.

Katrina tried to stop what was happening, and to break free of the almost bruising pressure of his kiss and pull away from him, but her lips were clinging eagerly to his, parting hotly for the hard thrust of his tongue.

Sanity, logic, her normally alert sense of self-preservation had all somehow become subservient to the thrill of longing and excitement surging through her. Under her fingertips she could feel the crispness of his thick hair, the corded muscles of his neck and the warmth of his skin. He felt so male, and so dangerous. So why wasn't she pushing him away instead of burying her fingers in his hair and holding him closer whilst white-hot pleasure licked through her?

The bruising pressure of his kiss should have made her recoil from him but instead it was kicking up inside her hot flurries of urgent need.

As she twined her tongue against his she felt the immediate shudder that wrenched his body, and then he was pushing her backwards and down onto the soft nest of silk cushions that covered the divan. Her only and immediate response was to wind her arms possessively around him, holding him to her.

Fire licked along her veins, igniting the longing she had been fighting to resist. In her dreams she had known of a man like this, a man of fierce, raw passions, untameable and elemental, a man whose merest touch would arouse her senses in a thousand and one ways, just as Xander was arousing hers now. And in that one shockingly intimate dream she had felt the full power of her response to him. Just as she was doing now!

The hands that had gripped her arms had somehow slid beneath her as she fell onto the divan, supporting and protecting her.

He shouldn't be doing this, Xander knew that. But her refusal to believe him ignited emotions he could not control. Just how bitter pride and raging anger had fused together to produce the hot, male hunger he was feeling, he had no idea at all! But what he did know was that he was being driven by an elemental need to possess her as no other man had ever possessed her, to drive from her body's memory every image it possessed of any other man but him.

He lifted his free hand to cup her face, so that he could look down into her eyes and see there only his own image.

'Look at me!'

The harsh command compelled Katrina to look up into Xander's face. A quiver of totally female awareness of him ran sensually through her as he lifted lean fingers to brush her tumbled hair off her face.

If it had not been for the dark thread of anger she had heard running through his harsh words, she could almost have believed that there was something tender in the way he was touching her.

But the hard, demanding mouth claiming her own wasn't tender, yet her lips were responding to the sensation with a wanton eagerness. He parted their softness with the fierce drive of his tongue, whilst his weight pressed her deeper into the softness of the cushions.

The argument that had brought them to this place, and to this intimacy, had faded into insignificance. His actions were no longer dominated and driven by the fierce urgings of his pride and need to punish her, Xander recognised, but it was a brief fleeting recognition, swamped by the intensity of his body's need for her.

Katrina felt his hands on her body, removing the protective modesty of her clothes, but instead of trying to stop him she was twisting and turning eagerly, wanting to accommodate and assist his rapid despatch of the barriers to the touch of his hands on her flesh.

Only a thin mist of sunlight could penetrate the thick protective walls of the tent, but it was enough to gild her naked body, as though it had been brushed with gold dust. She saw Xander suddenly go very still as he stared down at her nakedness, and a small quiver of shyness and uncertainty ran through her. He was the first man who had ever seen her naked. The only man she had ever *wanted* to see her naked.

Uncertainly she looked up at him. There was a look in his eyes that sent a reaction jolting over her, which tightened her nipples and sent a fierce thrill of sensation coiling through the most intimate part of her. He hadn't even touched her and yet from the way her whole body was reacting he might just as well have run his fingertip around her jutting nipples and then moved lower to part the sensually swollen fleshy lips of her sex to find the eager, waiting need of her pulsing clitoris.

She wanted him, ached for him, hungered and longed for him, right now, right here… She made a soft, small sound of liquid arousal, and immediately dark colour ran up under the taut flesh of Xander's jaw. He pulled off his own clothes, scarcely giving her time for more than a blurred glimpse of honey-gold skin over powerful male muscles, and a dizzyingly tempting covering of silky dark hair that fanned out over his chest, arrowing downwards over his taut belly, before he reached for her.

The feel of Katrina in his arms was doing something to him he had never imagined *any* woman could do, much less this one, Xander acknowledged as he gave into the urgency of his need to fill his waiting senses with the scent, and feel, and taste of her.

The silk cushions heaped on the divan felt decadently sensuous against her naked skin, but more dangerously erotic and sensual by far was the feel of Xander's naked body against her own, Katrina recognised breathlessly. The feel of his skin against hers was surely the closest she was ever likely to get to heaven, she decided headily as she gave in to the pleasure of running her hands possessively over his shoulders, stroking his flesh as she did so, closing her eyes, in order to savour and relish the feel of him.

If she never touched him like this again she would remember for the rest of her life how he had felt, how she had touched him; she was creating a precious visual image of him on which she could imprint everything her senses were relating to her. His scent, his arousal overwhelming the cool cologne he always wore so that she was acutely aware of the raw, musky, pheromone-drenched maleness of him, and of how his skin felt hot and sleek, the powerful definition of his muscles beneath it giving her a small, sharp female thrill of recognition of his strength, and of his arousal. She hadn't touched him intimately yet, but she could feel the hot, swollen length of his penis pressing against her own flesh, and that thrilled her in some nameless female way that still had the power to shock her and to challenge her own beliefs about herself.

What bemused her even more was that she wanted desperately to touch him there, to explore and know him. To feel him grow even harder and more urgent beneath her touch, and that alone should have been enough to shock her, because she had certainly never experienced such a feeling before.

But analysing her thoughts and feelings was way beyond her now. Xander had taken possession of her mouth, his tongue thrusting hotly past her lips as he demanded entrance. His hands cupped her breasts, holding them as though he was savouring the feel of the rounded globes of flesh, but then his tongue drove deeper within her mouth and his fingers kneaded her breasts, plucking sensuously at the stiff peaks of her nipples.

Unable to help herself, Katrina writhed hotly against him, her skin suffused with the flush of her own desire.

Looking down at her as she arched into his hands, her eyes closed as she moaned her desire, Xander realised that the feeling taking possession of him was a fierce need to ensure that the only man her body would ever recognise or remember as its lover was him! He wanted, no, *needed* to put his own personal imprint on her in such a way that she would never, ever forget him.

He bent his head to her breast, flicking his tongue tip against her hard nipple. Immediately Katrina cried out to him. She was oblivious to the fact that her nails were digging into the smooth flesh of his shoulders, and that she was lifting her hips to press her lower body even closer to the hard length of his erection, frantically rubbing herself rhythmically against him as she sought an easing of the pulsing ache possessing her own body.

Her wantonness was destroying him, Xander recognised on a surge of mingled arousal and anger. Every sensual movement of her experienced, eager body was inciting a matching response within his own.

'Xander, I want you so badly.'

The choked words were whispered against his ear, the same ear that her hot, pointed tongue was hungrily exploring.

His self-control wasn't slipping away from him, it was exploding in a frenzy of white-hot lust.

'You're going to have me,' he answered her thickly. 'All of me. And I'm going to have you. I'm going to have you and fill you, and make you feel as no other man has ever done or will ever do... Is that what you want?'

'Yes. Oh, yes,' Katrina moaned. She who would have said anything, done anything he asked, she wanted him so much.

His hand was parting her thighs, stroking her soft, silky skin and making her quiver with the intensity of her longing.

He cupped her sex, parting her swollen outer lips, and rubbing one tormenting fingertip over her eager wetness. She heard the thick sound of satisfaction he made when he stroked the hard, erect flesh of her clitoris, his fingertip moving erotically over it, and arousing her to such a fever pitch of desire that she could hardly endure the intensity of her own pleasure.

Xander could hear the small quiet voice inside himself telling him what he was doing was wrong, but its warning was drowned out by the small excited sounds Katrina was making and his own intense desire.

He had never wanted a woman as he wanted this one, nor had he ever known he could feel such an overwhelming and passionate need. He could feel it driving, burning through him, possessing him as he ached to possess Katrina.

He positioned himself between her already open, welcoming thighs. Katrina shuddered. She could see Xander poised over her, and her heart hammered frantically against her ribs. This was it. The moment of intimacy she had wondered about, dreamed about with a virginal mixture of eager curiosity and slight trepidation.

She could feel Xander's muscles bunching. Almost pleadingly she lifted her hand to his face, whispering chokily, 'Kiss me…'

Swiftly Xander bent his head, his mouth taking hers in a long, slow kiss of scorching intimacy whilst he thrust fiercely past the swollen outer lips of her sex, and into the tight embrace of the most intimate part of her.

And she did feel tight, the close grip of her muscles almost unendurably erotic.

Foolishly, perhaps, she hadn't expected pain, Katrina acknowledged as her body clenched in shock, but her longing for him was stronger than both her shock and her pain. She clung to him, offering herself up to him, so that he thrust deeper and faster.

He felt the barrier of her virginity and heard her indrawn gasp of pain with a shock wave of stunned disbelief.

Katrina shuddered as his body stilled within hers; the pain had gone but the small, telling contractions pulsing deep inside her had not. They were intensifying, making her move rhythmically and urgently against Xander, compelling him to move with her.

She heard him groan, her own teeth nipping frantically at his shoulder as the urgency of her arousal seized her and she cried out to him in agonised pleasure. The deep, driving surge of his body within her own was all pleasure now and she gave herself up to it and to him, lost in what she was experiencing, the release of her orgasm making her tremble from head to foot. But it was the hot spill of Xander's completion within her that made her eyes burn with emotional tears.

On a small sigh of soft pleasure she turned her face into the curve of Xander's shoulder and curled up against him.

'How is it possible that you were a virgin?'

The harsh, angry words confused her.

'So far as I know there is only one way I could have been,' she responded flippantly.

What did it matter what she had been when right now she was gloriously, deliciously, totally fulfilled and by him?

'It isn't exactly unknown for women to buy themselves virginity via a skilled surgeon and a small operation,' Xander told her curtly.

'Maybe it isn't, but I certainly didn't,' Katrina told him.

Xander knew that she had done no such thing, but he was still fighting to overcome his own shock. Discovering that she had been a virgin and he her first and only lover changed everything. His upbring-

ing meant that he felt a moral responsibility towards
her. 'You should have told me.'

He sounded cold and angry, and to her own chagrin
Katrina discovered that, instead of feeling blissfully
happy, suddenly she felt totally miserable and dangerously close to tears.

'I did tell you that Richard wasn't my lover,' she
reminded him.

'You could have asked me to stop.' He paused, an
expression crossing his face that Katrina couldn't analyse. 'By the time I recognised that I needed to stop,
it was far too late,' he added curtly.

He was criticising her for what had happened.
Blaming her? Despite her immediate indignation and
anger, Katrina knew that he had a valid point. She
could have told him, but she had deliberately chosen
not to do so! Why? Because she had intuitively
known that he would not continue to make love to
her? Because she had wanted him to do so, so desperately? Even so! Beneath the anger she was beginning to feel a very much deeper and more painful
current of emotional misery that was slowly flooding
her: a combination of rejection, despair, and the bleak
realisation that her own emotional input into their sexual intimacy had not been reciprocated. A small
shiver shook her still-naked body.

'Here, put this on.'

Katrina tensed as he wrapped his own discarded
robe around her. He was frowning as she did so, his
actions brisk and businesslike, and surely devoid of
any kind of softening tenderness, even if his touch
was surprisingly gentle.

'You realise, of course, that this changes everything

between us! Had I known of your virginity I would never—'

Katrina fought back the tears burning the backs of her eyes. 'Do you realise just how despicable you are?' she demanded hotly. 'You believed that…when you assumed that I had…that I was not…' She was so overwrought that she could hardly get the words out. Taking a deep breath, she started again. 'When you assumed I was Richard's lover, you obviously thought that it was perfectly acceptable for you to…to do what you did, but now that you've discovered that I was a virgin, things are different. Well, you may feel differently about me, but I do not feel differently about you!' she told him furiously. 'In fact, if anything I despise you now even more than I did before! The kind of man I could respect is a man who values me as a person, not just my virginity! You are despicable and loathsome!'

She could see the dark tide of angry colour seeping up under his skin, and the murderous flash of savage pride in his eyes, but she refused to be daunted. She had as much right to say what she thought as he did! She felt sick inside with shame and self-contempt at having been foolish enough to believe he was someone special. She had deluded herself, and now she had paid the price for that self-delusion—not with her virginity, but with her heart and her emotions.

At least now she would be able to destroy that burgeoning love by reminding herself of what had happened today and his cruelty towards her.

Her angry words caught Xander unprepared, just as his desire for her had done. They touched an exposed nerve and threw back to him an image of himself that hurt his pride.

He had lied to her when he had claimed that he had only made love to her because he had believed she was experienced. The truth was that he had made love to her because he had not been able to stop himself, but he had been too proud to admit that to her, and now it was too late to tell her that truth. It was also too late to admonish himself now for the fact that he had not taken any kind of precautions.

Healthwise he had no concerns. Despite what other people might choose to think about his sexual past, he was not littered with a stream of different partners, but there were other dangers, other risks, and he had not held himself back in any way at all!

He looked at Katrina. Her small heart-shaped face looked pale, her eyes huge.

Although the garment was wrapped around her, she was still shivering slightly.

Abruptly he stood up and then, grimly and without saying a word to her, he scooped Katrina up into his arms, fabric and all.

'What are you doing? Put me down!' Katrina commanded uselessly as he carried her through to the inner quarters of the tent.

Panic filled her. What was he going to do? But instead of turning into the sleeping area, he turned instead into the small bathroom. He pushed open the shower door with his shoulder and stepped into it, still holding her.

As he put her down he removed the cloth that was wrapped around her and dropped it on the floor outside the shower, firmly closing the door.

'What do you think you are doing?' Her question

was lost as he turned on the shower and she sputtered helplessly under the admittedly delicious warmth of the water.

'You're cold and possibly even slightly in shock,' he told her grimly. It was true that she did feel rather shaky, Katrina acknowledged, but she knew that that had more to do with Xander's angry comments to her than the intimacy they had shared.

She risked a small upward look at him. Xander might be soaping her wet skin with a look on his face that said there was nothing remotely sexual or pleasurable for him about what he was doing, but unfortunately her body was not capable of being so detached, Katrina recognised guiltily.

And of course it didn't help that he was as naked as she was herself. Unable to stop herself, she glanced down at his body, and then tensed as she saw that his penis was not small and flaccid as she had assumed naively it would be, but instead impressively thick and firm-looking.

A small perplexed frown creased her forehead.

'What's the matter?'

Her face burned with embarrassed colour. She hadn't realised that Xander was watching her so closely.

'Nothing. That is…I just thought…' she began in a suffocated voice, her face burning even more as he too looked at his own body.

'You thought what?' he challenged her coolly. 'That I might be planning to take you back to bed?'

'No!' Katrina denied immediately and truthfully, even though the distressing sudden tightening of her nipples told her how favourably her body was already viewing that possibility.

'No? Then what were you thinking?'

He was going to insist on her telling him the truth, Katrina recognised.

'I just thought that you…that after sex… You just looked much bigger than I'd imagined,' she finally blurted out uncomfortably.

'Imagined?'

The silky, challenging word caught her off guard, conjuring up the erotic thoughts and fantasies she had mentally created around him and rendering her tongue-tied and speechless.

Xander leaned forward, stroking the soapy sponge the length of her back, all the way down to the firm curve of her buttocks.

'So what exactly was it that you did imagine?' he asked her softly.

'Nothing,' Katrina denied quickly.

He dropped the sponge and looked at her, his intent, speculative gaze searching her face.

'Whilst men, like women, are all basically made the same, within the parameters of that sameness there are many different sizes, which is just one of the reasons why you should have told me that you were a virgin.'

He rinsed off the soap with the spray of the shower.

'I am surprised that your parents, your mother, and especially your father did not warn you about this kind of situation…'

'I do not have a mother or a father,' Katrina checked him quietly. 'They were killed in an accident when I was in my teens.'

'An accident?'

'They were scientists,' Katrina explained. 'They

were working on an ecological site in Turkey when a roof fell in on them.'

She heard the hiss of his indrawn breath.

'There is no need for you to feel sorry for me. I don't want anyone's pity. I am just glad that they died together, and I am so grateful for the love they gave me and the love they had for one another.'

She spoke with a quiet dignity that once again touched a raw, intimate place in Xander's own emotions. He had to fight against a sudden desire to put his arms around her and simply hold her.

'Stay here,' he said curtly instead, turning off the shower and stepping out, returning almost immediately with a huge soft towel that he wrapped firmly around her.

When she touched its softness with appreciative fingers he told her authoritatively, 'It's Egyptian cotton, and far superior to any other kind.'

'And far more expensive,' Katrina answered him ruefully before tensing and remembering just what he was.

But of course he had acquired the towels in the same way as he had acquired the books but, remembering the outcome of her accusations regarding them, she decided not to challenge him a second time.

Having wrapped her in one of the towels, he wrapped one around his waist and then started to rub her dry—more briskly than passionately, she had to admit. His self-imposed task completed, he wrapped her in a fresh dry towel and swung her into his arms.

'I can walk, you know,' she objected crossly, but she might just as well not have spoken for all the attention he paid to her.

In the close confines of the narrow corridor she

could smell the clean, soap-fresh scent of his skin. Her heart thumped heavily and then skidded against the bottom of her chest cavity. She badly wanted to press her lips against the smooth brown column of his throat and then to lick and nibble her way towards his mouth.

A now-familiar feeling of sensual tension was already starting to build again inside her. What had he done to her? Katrina wondered helplessly. How had he turned her from a naive virgin into a woman of wanton hungers and needs who was aching for him again already?

She told herself that it was relief she felt when he carried her into the sleeping area and placed her on the bed.

'Rest now,' he said.

'I don't need to rest,' Katrina objected immediately. 'Just because I was a virgin that does not mean I'm delicate.'

He had been about to turn away from her, but now he stopped and turned to look at her instead, sliding one long, lean-fingered hand against her throat so that she was forced to look back at him.

'You may have been a virgin but, admit it, you were eager and ready for me, weren't you?'

An expression she couldn't define, but which her body obviously understood, crossed his face, causing a small reactionary shiver of sensual excitement to grip her, but she still compressed her mouth and tried to look away from him.

'Answer me,' he insisted. The hard pad of his thumb was rubbing dangerously against her lips. She could feel them swelling sensitively against his touch and she ached to part them and taste the teasing thumb that was causing her so much torment.

'Answer me,' he repeated, removing his thumb.

'Very well. Yes, I was. You are obviously an experienced lover,' she told him colourlessly, determined not to let him see how she really felt.

'You will be in a far better position to know exactly how experienced by tomorrow's sunrise,' he told her mockingly. 'You have scarcely begun to know what sensual pleasure is, although I confess you are an extremely receptive pupil. Just now, in the shower, you looked at me as though you were as hungry for me as a woman of much greater experience. Have you any idea just how enticing and erotic it is for a woman to show a man how receptive she is to him?'

'I did no such thing!' Katrina objected, hot-faced.

'Liar!' he stopped her softly. 'Rest now, and tonight I will show you what pleasure really is.'

His arrogance was unbelievable, Katrina decided angrily, but underneath her anger she could feel the fierce, excited pulse of her own arousal. What she was allowing to happen was far too dangerous, she knew that, but somehow she just could not help herself.

She should hate and loathe him and not love him; she should...

Love him? She did not love him. She could not love him. What treachery had put that word into her head? She might want him. She might be excited by him, aroused and tantalised by him; she might be all those things and even a great deal more, but she did not love him!

CHAPTER EIGHT

MOROSELY Xander stared out across the oasis, beyond which the sun was dying fast towards the horizon.

By rights his sole concern, his every single thought, should have been for his half-brother, and the fact that tomorrow was Zuran's National Day, and the day Nazir had selected for his murder of the Ruler and his *coup d'état*.

But instead of focusing on that, his thoughts, and even worse his emotions, were rebelliously preoccupied with Katrina.

He had said and done things to her that were totally alien to his normal mode of behaviour, and that alone was enough to fill him with an explosive mix of anger and disbelief, without the additional discomfiting knowledge that he was now aching physically for her so intensely that he actually wanted to put into effect the ridiculous sexual boast he had made earlier. What on earth had prompted him to say such a thing? Surely he wasn't really so vain and shallow that just the wide-eyed, slightly awed and disbelieving way she had looked at his sex earlier had made him want to hear her make those little whimpers of pleasure all over again.

Where the hell were those agents? They should have returned by now with a formal warrant for Nazir's arrest and detainment. He was beginning to fear that they might not return in time. Which meant that he would have to find a way of stopping Nazir himself.

Xander's mouth compressed, a grim look darkening his eyes as Nazir strolled out from between the rows of tents, heading in the direction of the oasis.

Immediately Xander started to turn away from him, but, as though Nazir had somehow sensed his desire not to be noticed, Xander heard him call out sharply to him, 'You! Come here!'

Pretending not to have heard him, Xander started to walk away.

'Stop, or I shall shoot you.'

They were alone in the small palm grove, and Xander knew better than to delude himself that Nazir would not carry out his threat.

His own hand went automatically to the dagger in his belt. Like all the male members of the ruling family, he had undergone military training, but he had never killed anyone, nor imagined that he would have to. But now it seemed that fate was putting him in a position where he would have no option. If he ignored Nazir's demand Nazir would shoot him as he had threatened. And if he obeyed him then Nazir would no doubt quickly discover his real identity, and would guess that his plot had been discovered.

Taking hold of his dagger within the concealing folds of his clothes, Xander turned round to confront his half-cousin.

'You took too long, Tuareg.' Nazir was sneering. 'Perhaps I should kill you anyway.'

The gun was already in his hand and he was pointing it right at Xander's heart.

*   *   *

Katrina took a deep breath and stepped out of the tent. She had to find Xander and make him agree to release her. She had spent virtually the whole of the afternoon going over and over what had happened between them and she was acutely aware of how vulnerable to him she was.

That frightening word 'love', which had crept into her thoughts earlier, had lodged painfully in her heart, making her sickeningly aware of her own danger. She hated the thought of lowering her pride and pleading with him, but she had no other option. She had made up her mind that she was going to ask him how much ransom he intended to demand for her and somehow she would find a way to raise the money herself. She had the small house in England her parents had left her. Surely she could raise some money on that?

She had waited as patiently as she could for him to return, but now her patience had run out, and so she had decided to go and look for him. Soon it would be dark, and once she was alone with him in the intimacy of the tent with the sensual weight of the words he had said earlier still hanging on the air she was afraid that she might weaken.

It had been more instinct than anything else that had drawn her down to the oasis. And now she stood frozen in shocked fear as she witnessed what was happening.

The man pointing the gun at Xander had an obvious air of authority about him, and it crossed her mind that he might have come to the oasis in search of her, alerted to her plight by Richard.

Xander was standing still several yards away from the other man.

'Come closer,' Katrina heard the other man order sharply.

Her heart was thudding frantically against her ribs and a feeling of pain and anxiety was wrenching at her insides. Xander was a thief, and a kidnapper, she reminded herself. She owed him no loyalty whatsoever.

Xander still hadn't moved.

'You dare to disobey me, Tuareg? Very well, then.' There was a malevolent pleasure in the man's voice as he pulled back the trigger.

He was going to shoot Xander... Kill him!

Franatically Katrina rushed forward protesting emotionally, 'No...'

Both men turned towards her, Xander's harsh, 'Katrina!' leaving his lips at the same time as he flung himself towards her, but it was already too late. As fast as he was, he could not match the speed of a bullet.

Katrina felt it hit her with a sense of disbelief and bewilderment, which immediately became an intense, obliterating pain.

She could see Xander looking at her, his lips moving as he spoke to her, but the pain would not let her answer. It was clawing and tearing at her, dragging her away to its dark, cold lair. But at least Xander was safe and the man had not killed him.

Her last thought as she lost consciousness was one of confused awareness that Xander was holding her. But not even the warmth of his arms was enough to stop the icy cold that was filling her veins and stealing her away from him.

CHAPTER NINE

'KATRINA?'

Reluctantly Katrina opened her eyes and looked up into the face of the uniformed nurse smiling down at her. Katrina's mouth was dry and she felt heavy-headed, unable to think properly or clearly. Confusing images filled her slow-moving thoughts.

She was lying in what was obviously a hospital bed, but the room she was in was like no hospital room she had ever seen or imagined seeing. It looked more like a super-luxurious hotel bedroom: a sparkling clean, luxurious hotel bedroom, she acknowledged as she tried to sit up.

Immediately the nurse shook her head and showed Katrina a small but very complicated-looking remote-control device.

'You can alter the position of your bed with this,' she instructed Katrina, before adding, 'The doctor will be in to see you soon. Are you in any pain? You were given an intravenous painkiller after the operation last night to remove the bullet from your arm.'

The bullet! Agitation filled her as everything came rushing back to her. Xander. The desert. The man with the gun. Xander…Xander…Xander…

'Where am I? Where is…?'

'You are in the special private royal ward of the Zuran Hospital,' the nurse answered her importantly, plainly impressed with the status that Katrina had been accorded. 'The Ruler himself has told the chief

134

surgeon that he wishes to be informed of your progress hourly, and the Sheikha, Her Highness, the Ruler's wife herself will be visiting you this morning. We've received a gift of some clothes for you to wear when Her Highness comes to see you. You cannot receive Her Highness in what you were wearing when you were brought in to us. It would be a disgrace!'

The royal ward of Zuran Hospital? What was she doing here? How had she got here? She had no memory of anything after the explosion of pain she had experienced when she had been shot.

'Let me pour you some water,' the nurse offered. 'You must drink as much as you can to wash the anaesthetic from your system and to prevent you from becoming dehydrated.'

Katrina's eyes widened as she saw that the bottle of water she removed from the discreetly hidden fridge bore a royal crest, and her eyes widened even more when the nurse produced a heavily cut crystal tumbler for her to drink from.

But even as she gulped eagerly at the crystal-clear cool water it wasn't her own situation that was on her mind so much as Xander's. Where was he?

'The man,' she began hesitantly, but the nurse stopped her immediately, a look of contempt and anger darkening her eyes.

'He has been taken into custody by the special agents from the Ruling Council. By good fortune they had arrived at the desert camp of the renegade El Khalid in time to witness everything. Indeed it is thanks to them that you were brought immediately here to Zuran. The Council will decide on the ultimate fate of this unspeakable villain, but there is no doubt that he will receive his just deserts. Such a man truly deserves to be punished for what he has done!'

Katrina's heart sank lower with every word the other girl uttered. 'Where is he now?' Katrina asked her chokily. Her drug-fogged brain was already planning recklessly to plead Xander's case, and to beg for mercy to be extended to him. Wildly Katrina wondered how much money she could borrow against her small home and if it would be sufficient to buy Xander his freedom.

She was halfway to working out the details of such a plan when she realised abruptly what her frantic thoughts meant.

She had told herself that she did not love Xander, but why else would she be feeling the way she was? Surely a much more appropriate emotion ought to be more of relief at having finally escaped from him. She should feel determined to put everything that had happened to her and Xander right out of her mind for ever. But instead she was making desperate plans to help him!

'The special agents from the Ruling Council have taken custody of him in prison and he will be held there until his trial. His Highness made an announcement to the nation this morning to alert us to what has been happening, and of the bravery of his half-brother Sheikh Allessandro, who was the one who discovered the plot against the Ruler. Sheikh Allessandro is to join His Highness in his walkabout today during our National Day celebrations. I will put the television on for you and you will be able to watch the celebrations,' the nurse told her enthusiastically, beaming with delight.

Katrina felt too sick with despair to respond. She

tried to remind herself that she had known all along
what Xander was, and how much his moral outlook
on life differed from her own. She had warned herself
of the emotional danger she'd been in and how foolish it would be for her to allow herself to weave
dreams and fantasies around him, but she might as
well not have bothered! Stupidly she had done exactly
what she had told herself she must not do!

Where was Xander now? Was he already incarcer-
ated in some cramped prison cell? She tried to imagine the proud features contorted with fear, but she
could not do so. The image of him that was burned
for ever in her memory was that of him standing tall
and magnificent before her.

'What…what will they charge him with?' she
asked the nurse huskily.

'Treason—he dared to threaten the life of our beloved Ruler,' the other girl responded darkly.

Katrina made a small sound of anguished protest,
but the nurse didn't hear it, she was too busy putting
the television on, her back turned towards Katrina.

As soon as the nurse had gone, the consultant himself
arrived. Katrina lay stiffly in the bed, consumed with
despair and anxiety for Xander, whilst the consultant
inspected the wound to her arm.

'You are a very fortunate young woman,' he told
Katrina benignly. 'Another few centimetres and the
bullet would have penetrated your heart. Mind you,
you are not alone in your good fortune, for I would
not have cared to have to inform His Highness that
you were seriously injured. He was beside himself
with anxiety for you.'

He was trying to be amiable, Katrina realised, forcing herself to try to smile in response to his jocular comments.

'Excellent,' he pronounced when he'd finished examining her wound. 'I do not think we need have any concerns about your ultimate full recovery. You have had a lucky escape!'

She might have had a lucky escape, but Xander had not escaped, had he?

Every particle of her ached with anxiety for him. She wanted to go to him, to be with him, to tell him that she would do everything she could to help him.

Every second she spent here in hospital was a second wasted, a second she could have spent helping Xander.

'When will I be able to leave?' she asked the consultant impatiently.

He pursed his lips consideringly before answering her, frowning slightly as he looked at her. 'Certainly not for at least another twenty-four hours. If there is some problem and you feel we have not taken proper care of you, then please do say so. I would not want His Highness to think you were not totally happy with the care you have received here.'

He looked so concerned that Katrina immediately felt a small twinge of guilt.

'It is not that,' she tried to reassure him. 'It is just...' She stopped and bit her lip. How could she explain to him why she was so anxious to leave?

His pager started to bleep, and he turned away from Katrina to answer it.

'Her Highness is on her way to see you,' he told Katrina. 'I shall send a nurse in immediately in order to help you to prepare for her visit.'

He had gone before Katrina could say anything.

His departure was followed almost immediately by the arrival of a young nurse, carrying several glossy carrier bags.

'We must be quick. We only have half an hour before Her Highness will arrive. I will run a bath for you, and we must of course keep the dressing on your arm dry.'

It was like being caught up in a small whirlwind, Katrina decided as she was gently but firmly escorted from her bed to an *en suite* bathroom of such luxury that she could only stare open-mouthed at it.

She tried to insist that she could manage by herself, but her self-appointed guardian took no notice, albeit discreetly turning her back when Katrina slipped out of her hospital gown and into her bath.

Ten minutes later she was engulfed in a thick snowy-white towel, her eyes blurred with anguished tears as she remembered another bathroom and another towel and Xander saying coolly to her that the finest towels were made from Egyptian cotton. Xander! She could hardly bear to think of the conditions under which he was probably being held, never mind contrast them to the luxury with which she was surrounded.

It seemed that for the Sheikha's visit protocol demanded that she must be fully dressed.

But she soon discovered that it was not her own clothes she was to wear, but instead she had to choose from the contents of the carrier bags that the nurse had spread out on the bed for her consideration.

'But these are expensive designer clothes,' Katrina protested. 'I cannot afford any of these.'

'They are a gift from Her Highness,' the nurse informed her, and then added anxiously as she saw

Katrina hesitate and frown, 'It would be an insult to Her Highness if you were to refuse her gift.'

Reluctantly Katrina picked up one of the outfits—a pair of cream trousers in a mixture of linen and silk, with a soft blouson-style long-sleeved matching top. It disturbed her a little to be handed a set of brand-new, obviously expensive, delicately embroidered cream silk underwear, knowing just how much it was likely to have cost and that ultimately she would want to insist on paying for it herself.

Even so the delicate fabric felt wonderful against her skin, whilst both the demi-cup bra and the minute low-waisted, short-cut briefs that clung seductively to her skin were a perfect fit, although they were a rather more sensual design than she would have chosen for herself. As she caught sight of her own reflection in the mirror the rounded shape of her breasts was enhanced by the bra, whilst the briefs emphasised the slender length of her legs and the curve of her bottom. She couldn't help thinking that she might have chosen them to wear for Xander.

'Quick, we must hurry. Her Highness will be here soon,' the nurse was urging her, and dutifully Katrina reached for the cream trousers.

She might be dressed, but obviously she was still not deemed to be ready, she recognised as the nurse guided her to the dressing table and asked her to sit.

'I will dry your hair for you,' she announced, producing a hair-dryer from the dressing-table cupboard and proceeding to dry Katrina's newly washed hair.

Katrina wanted to protest that she could dry her hair herself, but she was conscious of her injured and bandaged arm.

Ten minutes later, with her hair dry and sleekly

brushed, the nurse just had time to whisk away the brush and dryer before there was a knock on the door and another nurse hurried in to say that the Sheikha had arrived.

'She will receive you in the state waiting room,' Katrina was informed. 'We will escort you there.'

A hospital with a state waiting room! Just how cool was that? Katrina wondered ruefully as she was hurried from her own room, down a long, carpeted corridor to a door outside which the consultant was standing.

'Her Highness will receive you now,' he told Katrina, opening the door for her and then standing back.

Katrina's first thought was one of surprise that the Ruler's wife was so tiny. She was seated on a raised dais, and when she saw Katrina she beckoned her to enter the room.

Although she had not planned to do so, Katrina found herself automatically and instinctively bowing her head as she remembered the protocol she had learned before coming to Zuran. In the East, after all, the act of prostration was one of respect rather than one of subservience. But to her surprise as the door was closed, leaving them alone in the room, the Sheikha got up off her seat and indicated that Katrina was to rise.

Coming over to Katrina, she unclipped her veil and took hold of Katrina's hands in her own, leaning forward to kiss Katrina on first one cheek and then the other.

'We are so much in your debt,' she exclaimed so emotionally that Katrina felt slightly overwhelmed.

'I have done nothing, Your Highness. I—'

'Your modesty is very becoming, but unnecessary since I have already heard all that we owe you. Your arm is not troubling you too much, I hope? The surgeon says that you will make a full recovery and that there will not be any scar. His Highness instructed me to express to you his devout hope that you will forgive him for being the cause of your suffering. I cannot bear to think of what would have happened if that unspeakable wretch had been allowed to carry out his murderous plan!'

Katrina took a deep breath. It might be a breach of protocol, but she had to seize the chance to do what she could for Xander.

'Highness, if I might speak?' Without waiting for the Ruler's wife to respond, she plunged on. 'I know what Xander planned to do was a terrible thing, a truly dreadful thing, and I...I can well understand why...why he should be about to face trial, but if I could beg for him to be shown some clemency...? Truthfully I do not believe him to be an evil man, even though...' Katrina knew the risk she was taking and the extent to which she was breaking the unwritten rules governing protocol, but she had to try to help Xander. Fearful tears were burning the backs of her eyes. The Ruler's wife was frowning so much that Katrina dared not continue. Her mouth had gone dry with nervous tension and her heart was thudding against her chest wall.

'Xander?' the Sheikha demanded, an expression Katrina could not define crossing her face.

'So! You wish to plead for mercy for this... this... Xander?'

Numbly, Katrina nodded, not trusting herself to speak.

'I understand that you were kidnapped by El Khalid's men, and that you suffered a great deal of indignity at their hands. Surely instead of pleading for mercy for...one of them, you should be urging my husband to punish him most severely.'

Katrina bit her lip. 'I'm not saying he shouldn't be punished—just that the way he protected me should be taken into account at the trial.'

'I shall speak with my husband,' the Ruler's wife announced evenly, stepping back from Katrina to return to her seat.

'It seems you are compassionate as well as modest. These are excellent virtues in a wife...and a mother,' she informed Katrina, causing her to do a small double take as she heard the amusement in the Ruler's wife's voice and then saw as she secured her veil that she was smiling broadly as though something had amused her.

'I hope that this...this Xander is aware of what a passionate champion he has in you!' she murmured dryly. 'Indeed one might almost suppose that you had fallen in love with him!'

Ten minutes later, her audience over, Katrina was back in her own room, her stomach still churning with nervous tension. The television was still on, and she paused to glance at it. On the screen in front of her she could see the packed streets of Zuran City as people waited to cheer the Ruler as he walked amongst them.

Katrina knew that Zuran's Ruler was held in very high regard, not just by his people, but also by the international community and its leaders. He was considered to be a forward-thinking, modern-minded man who had done a great deal to improve the lives of his people. Thanks to his foresight and vision Zuran had become a major luxury holiday destination; his racing stable and the Zuran Cup race were world famous, as was the golf tournament he had instigated, and now there was talk of the country being added to the international formula one racing circuit.

How on earth had Xander become involved in a plot to depose such a highly thought-of man and, in doing so, to destabilise Zuran's political and economic situation?

She knew the answer to that question, she acknowledged bleakly. Xander would do anything for money. He had even gone through a fake marriage ceremony with her for it!

Why couldn't she despise him as she knew she ought to do, instead of despising herself for feeling the way she did about him?

She looked absently at the television screen. As well as the Ruler himself, several other obviously high-ranking men were accompanying him on his walkabout, and the television announcer was explaining who they were for the benefit of his viewers.

'His Highness is accompanied by several members of his family, the most important of whom of course is his half-brother and saviour, Sheikh Allessandro Bin Ahmeed Sayed. Sheikh Allessandro's mother, as many of our viewers will know, was originally His Highness's English governess before his esteemed father married her. It has always been known that a tremendous closeness exists between His Highness and his younger half-brother. But now this bond has been intensified a thousand thousand times with the

Sheikh's bold action in personally seeking out His
Highness's would-be assassin.

'And there is Sheikh Allessandro now, standing on
the right of our esteemed Ruler.'

Bitterly Katrina reached for the remote. She did not
want to see the man who had put Xander in prison,
but it was too late. The camera had zoomed in on the
face of the man standing beside the Ruler of Zuran.

And it was a face as familiar to her now as her
own!

Rigid with shock and disbelief, Katrina stared fix-
edly at the screen, 'Xander!' she whispered numbly
in shocked denial. It couldn't be! But it was!

The man standing beside the Ruler, the man the
commentator was describing in such glowing,
admiring terms…the man he had named Sheikh
Allessandro, and half-brother to the Ruler, was
Xander!

She blinked and refocused on the screen, half convinced she must have been hallucinating, but, no, she
wasn't. Xander was not imprisoned in some horrid
jail, but instead walking freely through the streets of
Zuran, being heaped with praise and admiration.
Xander was not a penniless Tuareg nomad, he was an
extremely wealthy man. But he was a liar and a thief.
He had lied to her deliberately and knowingly, and
he had stolen from her too. He had stolen her heart.

No wonder the Ruler's wife had laughed when
Katrina had pleaded for leniency for him.

Her whole body burned with painful self-contempt
and bitterness. No doubt Xander would be richly
amused when he learned of her concern for him!

Angrily she stabbed at the remote and switched off the television.

Well, Xander could laugh as much as he liked; she would be on the other side of the world and too far away to hear him! She was going home to where she belonged and she was going right now! She pressed the bell to summon a nurse. She had left her handbag in Richard's car and her passport and credit cards had been in it so she would have to call at the small office he rented to collect them, and then she would go straight from there to the airport and she would stay there until she got a seat on a plane to take her back to England.

When the nurse arrived Katrina told her shakily, 'I would like my clothes, please. The ones I was wearing when I arrived? And I need to order a taxi, please.'

The nurse looked confused. 'A taxi? But you cannot leave the hospital until you have been discharged.'

Katrina lifted her chin. 'I am discharging myself. My clothes?' she reminded the other girl.

'I…I shall go and look for them for you,' the nurse said.

It might be as well to telephone Richard to warn him that she was on her way, Katrina acknowledged. That way he could have her personal papers ready for her. And perhaps she should ring the airport as well to find out when the next flight was.

It seemed a very long time before the nurse finally arrived back with her clothes.

'A car has been arranged for you,' she told Katrina. 'But the consultant should see you before you leave.'

'No! I do not need to see him. I am fine. Thank

you for bringing my clothes,' Katrina said to her gruffly.

She could see that the nurse wasn't entirely happy with the situation, but to Katrina's relief she did not try to argue with her or dissuade her.

Ten minutes later, Katrina was standing in the hospital's elegant reception area, feeling far weaker than she wanted to admit.

'I asked if a taxi could be ordered for me?' she said to the girl behind the reception desk.

'Oh!' For some reason the receptionist looked slightly flustered, glancing towards the smoked glass doors almost anxiously before telling Katrina, 'Yes. A limousine has been ordered and is waiting for you.'

A limousine! Ruefully Katrina acknowledged that it was unlikely that many of the hospital's patients had ever travelled in anything as mundane as a mere taxi. Thanking the girl, she made her way towards the exit. The doors swung open automatically, the brilliance of the sunlight dazzling her so much that she could hardly see.

Straight away, a highly polished black limousine with dark-tinted windows pulled up alongside her. The driver got out and bowed to her before opening the rear passenger door for her and then, after ensuring that she was comfortably settled, he resumed his own seat.

The car certainly was luxurious, Katrina reflected as she sank into its deep leather upholstery.

'I'm going to the airport,' she told the driver. 'I need to stop off somewhere first. L39 Bin Ahmed Street, please.'

A little to her surprise, the driver activated a glass

partition, which slid up to separate her from him, the faint clicking sound that followed it making her frown slightly as she recognised that the noise was the doors locking.

Perhaps he thought she looked like the kind of passenger who might try to get out without paying him, she decided ruefully as the car pulled out into the busy traffic.

Every taxi driver in Zuran City had to go through a rigorous training programme before he was given his licence, which included not only the ability to speak English, but also a thorough knowledge of the city's road system, and Katrina knew that her driver would know his way to the address she had given him.

There was a small nagging ache from the wound in her arm, and she realised that the painkillers she had been given every six hours in the hospital must be wearing off.

Despite the car's undeniable comfort and the coolness of the air-conditioning she began to feel slightly sick and shaky. A sign perhaps that physically she was not yet as fully recovered as she had believed?

She could visit her own doctor once she was home in England, she told herself stubbornly.

She had no idea how far the hospital was from the small office and accommodation the research team had been given to use, Katrina admitted, but it seemed to be taking a very long time for them to get there. They were travelling down an impressively straight dual carriageway. The central reservation and the verges either side were ornamented with an impressive formal display of plants, and the sea was on one side of the road while the desert was on the other.

Katrina began to frown. Had the driver mistaken her instructions and thought she wanted to go straight to the airport? She didn't remember the airport road looking like this, but it was obvious that a road so impressive had to lead somewhere important!

She leaned forward, tapping on the dark glass panel that separated her from the driver in an attempt to attract his attention, but to her frustration he did not respond.

Had he even heard her? The car started to slow down and she could see a huge wall rearing up in the desert ahead of them, stretching right across to the sea itself. Through the one-way dark glass she could see the sentries standing outside the ornate gold-coloured gates, ornamented with all manner of traditional designs picked out in dazzlingly vivid enamels.

It was like something out of an Arabian fairy tale, Katrina decided, bemused to see how the gates swung open as they approached, allowing them to sweep into the courtyard that lay beyond them.

More sentries guarded the imposing double doors, and the steps leading up to them by which the driver had brought the car to a halt.

Nervously Katrina stared out of the car at her unfamiliar surroundings. Where on earth was she, and more importantly what was she doing here? Katrina stiffened as the double doors opened and a man started to descend the steps. Xander!

One of the sentries leaped forward to open the car door before he could reach it, but it was his familiar hand that reached into the car and took hold of her arm as she automatically pressed herself back into the seat away from him.

'I'm not going anywhere with you,' she told him,

beginning to panic. 'So you can tell the driver to turn this car round and—'

'You have two choices, Katrina. Either you step out of the car willingly or…' He looked meaningfully at the impassive sentries standing several feet away.

Reluctantly Katrina got out of the car, casting a fulminatingly furious look at Xander as he ushered her towards and then up the flight of steps.

'You don't look well. It was extremely foolish of you to discharge yourself from the hospital. When the consultant telephoned me he was extremely concerned,' Xander announced as he guided her through the doors as they were flung open with faultless timing. They passed through them and into a cool, high-ceilinged room with an intricately carved staircase that led up to a gallery that ran the full length of the inner wall. Several doorways led off both the gallery and the ground floor, but Xander made no move towards any of them.

'The consultant had no right to discuss me with you,' Katrina told him.

'On the contrary, he had every right,' Xander corrected her. 'Since I am your husband!'

Katrina almost staggered with shock, as though she had been dealt a physical blow as well as an emotional one.

'That's not true,' she denied shakily.

'My brother chooses to think differently,' Xander informed her coolly. 'Especially now that his wife has spoken to him of a conversation she had with you during which you pleaded for me to be shown mercy and compassion—'

'That was before I realised that you weren't Xander, the thief, but Sheikh Allessandro, the liar,'

Katrina stopped him bitterly, still shocked that he'd heard about her conversation with the Sheikha.

'Come with me,' Xander said. 'The hallway of my brother's palace is not the place to discuss this!'

A palace! This place was a palace! She should perhaps have guessed, Katrina recognised, half dazed by the intensity of the conflicting emotions swamping her.

Xander had said he was her husband. But he wasn't. Not really. He couldn't be! Could he?

He had taken hold of her arm and she had no option other than to walk alongside him as he took her through one of the doors, and then along a long corridor, and then through a doorway, which opened out onto a small private garden.

As Katrina tried to focus on her surroundings through the blur of her angry tears she could hear Xander telling her grimly, 'This is my brother's private garden and he has allowed me the privilege of bringing you here so that we may talk in private.'

'We don't have anything private to talk about,' she shot back at him immediately.

'No? Why did you beg my sister-in-law to intervene on my behalf?'

'I'd have done the same for anyone I knew who I thought was going to face a harsh sentence. I thought you were a thief, but not a murderer. I didn't do it because of…of anything else! But of course you weren't facing treason charges, were you? Not that your sister-in-law told me that! No! I was left to find out when I saw you on television.'

She could feel and hear the bitterness and shock leaking from her heart into her voice.

'My sister-in-law pre-empted my own plans by visiting you before I could speak with you myself.' His voice was stiff—with regret or with lack of interest? It had to be lack of interest, Katrina decided.

'I couldn't say anything to you whilst we were in the desert,' he continued. 'I had to put my half-brother's safety first.'

'Your half-brother,' Katrina repeated bitterly. 'You even lied to me about that as well, didn't you?' When he remained silent she burst out, 'Do you really think I would really want to be married to someone like— a man who...who is everything I despise?'

She was shaking so badly she could hardly stand, but to her relief Xander had released her to turn away from her so that he couldn't see how agitated and distressed she was. 'Besides, you told me yourself that the ceremony we went through wasn't binding or legal. You are not my husband, Xander.'

'Unfortunately for us, it is not what you or I want that matters in Zuran. My brother is far from being a despot, but he does have certain beliefs, a certain stubbornness, if you wish to put it that way, that comes with being Ruler. He considers the traditions of our tribal ancestors to be a sacred trust, which he has a moral duty to respect. You and I were married according to one of those traditions and thus he feels...'

'How does he know that?' Katrina asked fiercely.

Caught up in her own feelings, Katrina was too agitated to notice Xander's small but telling hesitation before he answered her.

'El Khalid was held for questioning by Zuran's security forces.'

'And he told them? But such a ceremony can't possibly be legally binding!' Katrina protested.

'No, not in the eyes of the wider world, which is why my brother has arranged for us to go through a civil marriage ceremony discreetly and immediately.'

'No. No way, and what do you mean, "immediately"?' Katrina queried warily.

Xander inclined his head. 'I mean immediately,' he said evenly, ignoring the small sound of distress she made. 'The appropriate officials are waiting for us as we speak. My brother's wife has expressed her own disappointment that she cannot organise a more fitting ceremony for us—but my brother is adamant.'

'You can't do this! You had no right to bring me here! You can't make me marry you, Xander,' Katrina protested shakily. 'I am a British citizen and if I want to leave Zuran, which I do, I can right now...'

'According to Zuran law you are my wife, and as such a member of the Zurani royal family. No member of his family is allowed to leave the country without my brother's approval!'

Katrina stared at him. 'Why are you doing this?' she demanded in a shaken whisper. 'You must find the thought of a marriage between us as abhorrent as I do. You can't want to marry me any more than I want to marry you!'

'It is my duty to do as my brother commands me and, besides, since I took your virginity...' He gave her a look that made her stomach plunge nauseatingly.

'You're marrying me because of that! But that's... that's archaic...medieval...' Katrina protested in a distraught whisper.

'I will not have my child born without my name!'

Xander told her coldly. 'You are already my woman, now you must become my wife!'

Katrina's mouth had gone dry. 'What child?' she demanded recklessly. 'There isn't going to be any child,' she told him, looking deliberately at a point to one side of his shoulder instead of into his eyes. And then she held her breath, half expecting him to accuse her of lying, because the truth was that she could not say as yet whether or not she was carrying his child. To her relief, though, he didn't challenge her. Instead he simply told her curtly, 'Come…the officials are waiting.'

She didn't want to go. Apart from anything else, the pain in her arm had intensified to the point where she was having to grit her teeth against it. But the look on his face told her that he was all too likely to pick her up and carry her to her wedding bodily if she refused to walk there herself.

She was hardly dressed as a bride, Katrina admitted fifteen minutes later as she and Xander stood in front of the government official marrying them and legalising their desert ceremony. She certainly did not feel like one either. Neither did Xander look anything like a deliriously happy bridegroom.

He was reaching for her hand, as the official had instructed him to do, and to her chagrin it trembled frantically in his hold.

He had obviously come prepared because he produced a shiny new wedding ring to slide onto her ice-cold ring finger. Her fingers might be cold, but her arm was throbbing hotly and so was her head, Katrina acknowledged as she fought against the increasingly intense surges of pain washing over her.

'You may kiss the bride.'

Katrina felt herself shudder as she saw the dow[n]ward movement of the dark head. She closed he[r] eyes, not wanting to see Xander's face, not able to endure facing the reality of her own shattered dreams.

His lips barely touched her own. The kiss he was giving her was a parody of what a man's kiss for his new bride should have been. Pain, both emotional and physical, seized her, clawing and tearing at her as she tried to pull away.

'You are my wife, you will not recoil from me as though my touch is tainted,' she heard Xander hiss savagely against her ear.

Immediately she opened her eyes, bewildered both by his fury and his misinterpretation of her reaction. She snatched a brief glance at his face. It was set as hard as granite fused with marble—and just as cold and forbidding.

His hands were gripping her arms tightly and the pain in her injured one shot through her, making her cry out. But the sound was lost as Xander covered her mouth with his, taking it in a kiss of savage anger, his mouth burning her like a brand.

She could hear a buzzing in her ears, feel a dizziness in her head. Her body went weak and limp; only the grip of Xander's arms supported her as she slid into a dead faint.

CHAPTER TEN

KATRINA opened her eyes, and then moved her arm very cautiously. No pain!

'Good, you are awake. I will send someone to inform Xander. He is worrying himself sick and wearing out my new carpet by pacing the floor outside the women's quarters.'

Xander worrying himself sick about her! Katrina turned her head so that the Ruler's wife wouldn't see her expression.

'Our good chief consultant is very upset that you discharged yourself without his authority. He wanted to re-admit you to hospital but Xander wanted you to stay here.'

So that she couldn't escape from him, Katrina reflected dully.

'You should not be experiencing any pain now, because the consultant has seen to it that you have been given some medication, but if you are you must let me know and I shall tell Xander so that he can instruct the consultant to call and see you.'

'There isn't any pain,' Katrina told her woodenly. It wasn't true, of course. Her arm might not be hurting her, but the kind of pain she was now experiencing could not be cured by medical means, and would be with her for ever, she acknowledged.

'My husband is so pleased that Xander has finally met the right woman! A woman who loves him, and yet who understands the complexity of his mixed heritage,' the Sheikha announced.

Too late Katrina remembered the Sheikha's parting comment to her when she had visited her in hospital—about Katrina being a woman in love! Valiantly she tried to protect herself. 'I think there has been some mistake,' she began firmly, but immediately the Sheikha stopped her, saying gently, 'My husband, our beloved Ruler, does not make mistakes. He loves and knows what is best for all his family, but Xander has a special place in his heart. Not only is Xander his half-brother, but it was Xander's mother who taught my husband when he himself was young, when he was without a mother himself. It has long concerned him that Xander does not have a wife. But he knows he need not concern himself over Xander's marriage any longer!'

'That is all very well, but what about my feelings?' Katrina couldn't stop herself from protesting.

The Sheikha frowned slightly as she looked at her. 'But you love Xander,' she told Katrina. 'You pleaded with me to ask my husband to show him mercy!'

'That was before I knew who he was! He lied to me,' Katrina told her bitterly. 'He allowed me to think he was a…a thief and a…'

'He had no other option! It was his duty to put my husband's safety first,' the Sheikha continued. 'You should be proud of him for his loyalty to his brother and to Zuran. And besides, after hearing what happened at the oasis, my husband has decreed that your marriage must be legalised. As you are a young woman alone in our country my husband considers that you are under his protection, and naturally he is concerned to protect your reputation and act in your best interests. It would have been impossible for him to permit Xander to abandon you after what had happened. You have lived with him as his wife!'

'He told me that the ceremony meant nothing!' Katrina told her despairingly. But she could see that she was wasting her breath. In the Sheikha's eyes it was obviously unthinkable that she should not be legally married to Xander, and the woman was obviously relieved and grateful that she should be! But with her own eyes, all she could see was a future filled with pain and misery!

'Xander will be pleased that you are feeling better. He wishes to leave for the mountains tonight so that you can travel whilst it is cooler. I have instructed one of my maids to pack your things. I hope you like the clothes I had sent to the hospital for you. Xander will of course establish accounts for you with the designers of your choice once you return to Zuran. It is our custom that a newly married couple spend a month together on their own, getting to know one another, and I am sure you will love the villa in the mountains, which Xander's father left to him. He had it built for Xander's mother.'

Katrina wanted to protest that the only place she wanted to go was home to England, but she knew it would be no use.

Wearily she closed her eyes, wishing that there were a magic carpet on which she could fly away from the unwanted and unendurable life that lay ahead of her.

'You are quite sure you are well enough to travel?'

'The consultant has said so,' Katrina answered

Xander's curt question as they stood facing one another in the open courtyard where she had been taken to meet him by the Sheikha and her husband, Zuran's Ruler.

Katrina had been caught off guard by the Ruler's genuine display of warmth towards her, almost as though he was really pleased to welcome her into his family.

Now as he watched them he told Xander jovially, 'She is your wife now, Xander, and you may kiss her. In fact I would recommend that you do. The poor girl looks badly in need of some reassurance.'

'You are making her blush, my love,' the Sheikha joined in the conversation, linking her arm through his and smiling up at him as they dispensed with protocol and formality. 'Katrina is a very new bride and probably does not wish to share the tender intimacy of Xander's kiss with any onlookers.'

'Do you wish me to kiss you?' Xander asked Katrina promptly.

The Sheikha laughed. 'Oh, Xander. How very unromantic! Of course she does, but you must not expect her to tell you so!'

'Then she must wait for my kisses until she does,' Xander announced coolly. The Sheikha was still laughing, but Katrina felt more like crying. Her face was burning with a mixture of anger and humiliation and, although she hated admitting it even to herself, it would have been wonderfully comforting and reassuring to have Xander take her tenderly in his arms and hold her close. To have him whisper secretly to her that he loved and wanted her.

What foolishness was this? He was never, ever going to do that! And she suspected the only reason he had agreed to the convention of them spending a month together in private was so that he did not have to play the loving husband in public!

Xander might show her coldness and a lack of any kind of tenderness or loving emotion, but that was definitely not the way he behaved towards his family, Katrina noted. One by one, the Ruler's children presented themselves for a loving 'goodbye' hug from their uncle. And whilst he did not kiss the Sheikha, the warm, brotherly embrace he exchanged with her husband made Katrina feel very envious of their family closeness. No one watching them could dispute the strength of their love and respect for one another. But despite the love he had for Xander, the Ruler was still forcing his half-brother into a marriage he did not want, Katrina reminded herself.

'I pray your marriage will be a happy and a fruitful one,' the Sheikha told Katrina warmly as she embraced her. Her eyes burning with the pain of her unshed tears, Katrina tried to smile in response.

When the Sheikha released her Katrina saw that Xander was waiting. Wordlessly she walked with him across the courtyard. Two uniformed servants opened the gates for them, and Katrina caught her breath as she saw what was waiting for them in the much larger outer courtyard. There was not a car, as she'd expected, but a helicopter.

'We're travelling in that?' she asked Xander hesitantly.

'The villa is in the mountains and over twelve hours' drive away. You will be perfectly safe. I have held my pilot's licence for well over ten years and have never had an accident yet!'

'You will be flying the machine?' She couldn't control her surprise.

'I prefer to fly myself when I can.'

Silently Katrina digested his comments. There was so much about him that she did not know!

He was already striding towards the helicopter, obviously looking forward to flying it—no doubt far more than he was looking forward to his incarceration with her, Katrina reflected wryly as she hurried to catch up with him.

Katrina knew about the range of mountains inland and to the north of the city, but she had never imagined she would visit them, and certainly not under circumstances such as these.

Which reminded her… 'My colleagues—' she began.

'Their head office has been informed of your safety and our marriage.' His mouth hardened. 'Your colleagues returned to the UK within hours of your kidnap.'

'You forced them to return before the project was completed?' Katrina demanded angrily.

'I? I was in the desert with you, if you remember! The decision was made, I understand, following an urgent request from Richard claiming they wanted to return as he did not consider it safe for them to remain here following your kidnap.'

Katrina digested his information in silence. She had never liked Richard, but it still shocked her that he and the others had actually left the country without securing her own safety.

They had been travelling in darkness, the only illumination that of the stars against the inky dark sky and the thin sickle crescent of the new moon. Suddenly, up ahead of them, Katrina could see the illuminated sheer escarpment of what looked like a Moorish fortress, its turrets and fretted windows thrown into magical relief by the clever lighting.

'What's that?' she asked Xander, unable to contain her awe.

'That's our destination—the villa,' he answered calmly.

The villa? Unable to stop herself, she swung round to stare at him. 'That isn't a villa. It's…'

'It's the shell of a Saracen stronghold. My mother fell in love with the ruined building, apparently, and as a surprise for her my father had the villa built within the original outer walls. My parents spent as much time here as they could. It was their favourite home.'

They were starting to lose altitude as Xander skilfully brought the helicopter down over the escarpment, causing Katrina to hold her breath as they swept in over the high wall and then landed on the purpose-built helicopter pad within the ancient curtilage.

As soon as the blades had stopped rotating, servants seemed to appear from nowhere, hurrying to remove their luggage. But it was Xander himself who helped Katrina down from the helicopter, the cool strength of his hands on her skin making her ache inside with pain and longing and, even worse, remembered pleasure.

Quickly she pulled free of his grip, not wanting to be tortured by her body's memory of him any more than necessary.

Grimly Xander watched her, noting her averted profile and the way she recoiled from him.

He had tried to persuade his half-brother not to insist on this marriage, but he had been overruled. His
sister-in-law had told him that she was convinced that
Katrina loved him, and that, as much as anything else,
had swayed his half-brother's decision. Xander's
mouth compressed. Katrina did not love him. She
loathed him. She had told him so herself. Pain seized
him. When had he first started to love her? That first
afternoon in the souk when he had kissed her?
Certainly by the time Sulimen had tried to buy her
from him he had known that there was no power on
earth that would make him give her up. He had tried
to pretend it was not love that possessed him, just as
he had tried to tell himself that it was only his pride
that was badly hurt by the fact that she did not return
his feelings. Was he deluding himself in hoping that,
out of the compassion she had shown in pleading for
mercy towards him, love might grow?

Whether or not she grew to love him, as his brother
had reminded him, he had certain responsibilities both
towards her and towards his family.

As she walked with Xander from the outer courtyard
into the villa courtyard proper, it was impossible for
her not to feel awed and a little overwhelmed, Katrina
acknowledged as she paused to take in her surroundings. Within the shell of the ancient edifice, a villa of
such magical beauty had been created that she could
only gaze at it with a lump in her throat.

There was a garden within the ancient walls.
Discreet floodlighting revealed elegant waterways and
fountains, walkways and arbours, whilst the scent of
the flowers filled the night air.

'It's so beautiful,' she couldn't help whispering emotionally.

'My parents designed it together. My mother wanted it to be a perfect blending of east and west.'

His words were sharp and clipped, as though he resented having to speak to her, as though talking to her about his parents somehow contaminated them.

Did he really hate her so much?

Why should he not when he had been forced into a marriage with her that he did not want?

'The villa does not follow the traditional Zurani design,' Xander informed her as he put his hand on the small of her back to urge her forward. 'There are no separate women's and men's quarters.'

His touch caused a thrill of sensual pleasure and aching emotion to shoot through her. She wanted to turn round and beg him to take her fully in his arms, to hold her and kiss her and then to sweep her up and carry her to their bed. It must be the garden that was affecting her like this. She had no logical reason to want him and a hundred not to! But then love wasn't logical, was it? Love? She loved Xander? Really loved him? She trembled as violently as though she was experiencing a dreadful shock—or an unbearable truth!

'What is it? Is it your arm?' Xander demanded, frowning at her as he felt her trembling, but mercifully he had not realised that he himself was the cause of her reaction. 'Are you in pain?'

'No, I am just…tired, that's all.'

'I shall ask Miriam, the villa's housekeeper, to take you straight to your room. Dr Al Hajab has given me some painkillers for you.'

They were inside the villa now, standing in a

square hallway furnished with elegant simplicity in a pleasing mixture of Middle Eastern and western pieces of furniture set against pale blue colour-washed walls.

She could smell roses on the air, and everything about her surroundings breathed tranquillity and harmony, Katrina recognised. Inexplicably she felt as though someone had reached out and touched her with gentle lovingness, soothing her raw nerves and smoothing down her frayed emotional edges.

A sense of a weight being lifted from her shoulders stole softly through her.

'Ah, here is Miriam now!' Xander announced as a small and very rotund woman came hurrying excitedly towards them, and greeted Xander by flinging her arms around him. She was addressing him in terms of great affection in a flood of Zuranese spoken so fast Katrina struggled to understand what she was saying.

'Miriam, this is Katrina, my wife.'

Small, dark, shrewd eyes surveyed Katrina consideringly. 'Your mother would have liked her, I think.'

'Please take her to her room, Miriam. She is tired now, so you will have to wait until tomorrow to show her the rest of the villa.'

'A new bride and she is tired?' Miriam exclaimed forthrightly, making Katrina blush vividly.

'She has been injured,' Xander informed her evenly, before turning to Katrina and telling her, 'I shall leave you in Miriam's safe hands. I have some business to attend to, but if there is anything you want, then just tell Miriam and she will arrange it for you.'

Before she could say anything he was leaving, striding across the tiled floor and disappearing into a corridor.

'If you will follow me, please,' Miriam instructed Katrina, leading the way up the sweeping flight of marble stairs, and then across a wide landing to a pair of double doors, which she threw open almost theatrically, indicating that Katrina was to precede her into the room.

When she did, Katrina understood the reason for her small theatrical gesture, for the room she had walked into was unbelievably beautiful. Like the hallway, its walls were subtly colour-washed, this time in a shade somewhere between grey and a soft green that was infinitely relaxing to the senses. Priceless silk rugs warmed the cream marble of the floor, but it was the beautifully simple yet elegant Gustavian furniture that made Katrina gasp in delight. The wood was a slightly darker colour than the walls, the bed linen a cool off-white. The feeling of peace and harmony she had experienced earlier returned to her even more strongly and she had an overwhelming sense of a loving warmth that was not quite a presence and yet still very, very real for her.

'Was this Xander's mother's room?' she asked Miriam quietly.

The housekeeper nodded. 'The Sheikha chose everything for this villa herself. It was her special place, the only place where she could have the Ruler to herself. Do you sense her?'

'Yes,' Katrina acknowledged.

Miriam beamed. 'I knew it! I could tell the moment

you walked in that you were the right one for him. I was her maid,' she told Katrina quietly. 'I knew that she was carrying her child even before the Sheikh himself. She could not hide it from me! I was the one she wanted when she went into labour with him... She was so thrilled, so proud, to have given our Ruler a son. And she loved her baby so much! But then she became so very, very ill. She wanted so desperately to live, but it was not meant to be! Poor lady. She will be glad that you have married her son. You are of her own blood, and you love him, as she loved his father.'

It was a statement and not a question. Katrina didn't bother trying to argue.

'Your clothes have already been unpacked. I shall show you the dressing room and the bathroom and then I will leave you to sleep.'

Dutifully Katrina followed her into the dressing room, and then beyond it to a bathroom of such simple elegance that she sighed in mute pleasure. The room was fitted with plain white sanitary ware and the same Gustavian-style furniture as the bedroom and dressing room. There was a huge circular bath, half set into the floor, and beyond it floor-to-ceiling glass windows, which as Miriam demonstrated opened out onto a terrace. Beyond that, she explained, lay the small private garden that had been Xander's mother's personal retreat.

'I shall leave you now. Would you like me to send up something for you to eat...or drink?'

Tiredly Katrina shook her head. All she wanted was to shower the dust and grime of her journey off her skin and then to curl up in the bliss of her bed.

*   *   *

Xander opened the bedroom door and stood looking at the bed. The moonlight coming in through the patio windows revealed Katrina's sleeping form, her face turned towards him, her hair spread out over the pillow. Walking past her, he made his way silently through the dressing room to the bathroom, stripping off his clothes and turning on the shower.

He should not have allowed his half-brother to force him into this marriage to Katrina, he knew that. His sister-in-law might be firmly convinced that Katrina loved him, but he knew better. She did not love him, not as he wanted and needed her to do, with her heart and her soul as well as with her body. Physically she might have given herself to him, but that did not mean she loved him.

Even under the sting of the shower his body reacted immediately to the memory conjured up by his thoughts. Grimly he fought for self-control, turning the shower to cold and remaining under its icy lash until he was satisfied that he had subdued his physical yearning.

Stepping out of the shower, he reached for a towel and dried himself, and then padded naked back to the bedroom, pausing to look bleakly into Katrina's sleeping face. Her eyelashes made twin dark fans against her moon-pale skin, and she was so deeply asleep that even when he pulled back the bedcovers and got into the large bed, she didn't move.

Moonlight stroked the bare curve of her arm and the soft skin of her throat. He badly wanted to reach out and trace its silvered path, but he knew that if he gave in to that temptation he wouldn't be able to stop himself from taking her in his arms and kissing every delicious inch of her. Just as he had wanted to the first time he had seen her in the souk.

The stark reality of knowing that she did not love him as he did her cut into him with the slicing thrust of a dagger. Resolutely he turned away from her and put as much distance between them as he could.

CHAPTER ELEVEN

THE sound of crockery chinking and the rich smell of fresh coffee brought Katrina out of her sleep. Blinking a little against the dazzle of the morning sunlight, she looked in the direction where the discreet rattle of china was coming from. Beyond the now-open glass doors, which led onto the large terrace, she could see Miriam placing the crockery on a wrought-iron table.

On the point of throwing back the bed covers, she went completely still, her heart pounding heavily as she stared at the tell-tale indentation in the pillow next to her own, unable to drag her shocked glance away from it.

'So you are awake!' Miriam announced cheerfully, the sound of her voice finally breaking the horror of the realisation that she had not slept alone.

'I have instructed the staff to prepare for you the Sheikha's favourite breakfast! I hope you will like it!'

'I'm sure I shall, Miriam.' Katrina thanked her, trying not to feel uncomfortable as the housekeeper picked up her robe from the chair where she had left it.

Fortunately she had gone to bed wearing the newly washed nightdress that she had worn whilst in hospital instead of just sleeping in her skin as she preferred to do. The door to the dressing room suddenly opened and Katrina stiffened as Xander walked in. It was obvious that he had just had a shower. His hair was still damp and she could smell the clean, sharp scent of the soap he had used.

Still holding the robe, Miriam went over to him immediately, smiling broadly at him. Watching the affection with which he returned the older woman's hug, Katrina suffered a small pang of aloneness and exclusion.

'I thought you would like to have your breakfast on the terrace this morning. Katrina will enjoy seeing your mother's garden.' She handed Katrina's robe to Xander, and then, turning back to the bed, she said, 'When you are ready, Katrina, I shall show you the whole of the villa. I hope you will love it as we do, but if there are any changes you wish to make...'

'I am sure there won't be, Miriam,' Katrina reassured her immediately, and was rewarded with an approving smile before the housekeeper left.

As soon as she had gone Katrina ignored the fierce pounding of her heart and looked determinedly at Xander. He was leaning against the wall still holding her robe. 'You didn't tell me that we would be sharing a bedroom.'

Eyeing her thoughtfully, Xander prised his shoulders away from the wall, and her impressionable gaze was immediately attracted by the sensual ripple of male muscles beneath bronzed skin. Her heart was thudding now, her own muscles clenching as a result of the betraying quiver of sensation stirring within her. She couldn't be aroused by the mere sight of him! She must not be!

'I didn't think it was necessary, given the fact that we are a newly married couple. It is normal in marriage, after all, for a husband and wife to share a bedroom and a bed. To have told Miriam that we would be sleeping in separate rooms would have been bound to give rise to unpleasant speculation and gossip.'

'Maybe so, but our marriage is not normal,' Katrina couldn't stop herself from pointing out.

'Not normal?' Xander queried silkily. 'What exactly do you mean by that?'

'I mean that most people marry because…because they love one another and want to be together.'

There was a definite and disturbing pause, at least so far as Katrina and her thudding heartbeat were concerned, before he questioned even more silkily, 'Aren't you omitting one vital ingredient from that recipe? Wouldn't you agree that it is true that most people who marry desire one another physically?' he demanded softly. Katrina could feel her face starting to burn. There was something about the way he was looking at her…

'Physical desire does play a part in marriage,' she managed to agree, hot-faced.

'And you would agree that there has been physical desire between us?'

Why was he doing this to her—forcing her to humiliate herself like this? What was he trying to prove? And to whom? She already knew exactly how she felt about him! 'That…that was a mistake,' she told him. She might know how she felt, but no way did she want him to have access to that knowledge!

'A mistake?' He was walking towards the bed and she could feel herself starting to tremble as small, fiery darts of an emotion that was not the anger or rejection that she should have been feeling shot through her.

'Giving me your virginity was a mistake? When

you cried out beneath me you cried out with pleasure.'

'No!' Katrina's response came out as a small moan of sound that was as much a denial of the intent she could read in his gaze as it was of the claim he had made.

'I say, "Yes", and I shall prove to you that I am right,' Xander insisted softly.

'No! What happened that night was just…it meant nothing to me.'

Just as she meant nothing to him, Katrina reminded herself. She couldn't bear the pain of seeing in his eyes that he knew of her foolish feelings, her yearning and longing for him and for his love.

'You are lying and I intend to prove it.'

That speed and sinuous stealth was all desert warrior, Katrina acknowledged helplessly. He had crossed the bedroom floor so quickly and was standing over her, his body blotting out the sunshine without her having the time to take any kind of evasive action.

'Don't you dare touch me!' she told him bravely, but she could see her words were not making any impact on him.

A cruel, mocking smile curled his mouth as he leaned down and whispered silkily, 'But I am going to touch you, and you are going to want me to. You are going to cry out to me to please you, to take you, and to satisfy you.'

He was already manacling her wrists within a steely hard grip, then lifting her flailing hands above her head and keeping them there as he bent lower. She did what she could to reject him, stiffening her entire body and turning her head away from him, willing her lips to stay firmly clamped together.

But it wasn't her lips that received the shockingly slow, sweet, drifting caress of his mouth, but the inner curve of her exposed arm.

Ripples of pleasure quivered through her arm, building swiftly to a crescendo of sensation that leapt from nerve ending to nerve ending. She could feel the longing tightening her breasts, and causing her nipples to harden into defiant indications of their eagerness to share in the sensual delight he was giving the sensitised flesh of her arm.

She might be wearing a nightdress, but its fragile double layer of gauzy silk did nothing to conceal the effect he was having on her body as her nipples thrust tormentedly against it.

He was still kissing the soft flesh of her arm, but her pleasure had now become an increasingly agonising ache to feel his mouth against other, more needy parts of her body. The lips she had been compressing together so tightly had now parted, and if Xander had cared to look into them he could have seen quite plainly the aroused heat shimmering in her eyes.

She longed to take hold of his dark head and pull it down against her so that she could not just taste his mouth, but also lose herself in the pleasure of the passion. The intensity of her feelings should have shocked her—instead it incited her!

'Are you sure you don't want this?'

The taunting question jerked her back to reality.

'Quite sure,' she hissed at him fiercely. What kind of man was he that he could do something like this?

He was kissing her neck, pinioning her wrists in the firm grip of one of his hands whilst the other slid the straps of her nightgown down off her shoulders. His fingertips whispered against her skin. His lips feathered tormentingly light kisses along the line of her nightdress. A small shudder broke through her self-control, desire and need carrying her swiftly with their fierce current. Her body tensed, quivering like a tightly drawn bow. She heard Xander mutter something. A curse, or a prayer, she couldn't tell which. Then his mouth was on her breast, taking it through the layers of her nightdress as though he needed the feel of her too much to wait. A feverish burst of exultation shot through her, increasing a hundredfold as she felt him tug the fabric of her nightdress lower, exposing her other breast and allowing him to transfer the sensual attention of his lips and tongue to its silky flesh and tightly hot nipple.

She started to exhale and then stopped, gasping aloud in protest as he lifted his mouth from her breast.

'What is it you want?' His voice sounded thick and raw; the look in his eyes when his gaze roved her semi-nakedness matched the need she could feel burning through her. Mutely she shook her head.

'Tell me!' he insisted. 'Is it this?'

He had released her hands and he was kissing the valley between her breasts, his mouth moving downwards over the flesh he was exposing as he pushed her nightdress lower and then lower still.

'This—do you want this?'

'Yes!' she responded in desperation.

His tongue tip rimmed her navel, and whilst she fought to control the wet heat of the pleasure gripping her, in one fluid movement he removed her nightdress completely, leaving every inch of her open to his sight and touch.

sight of his dark head bent over her naked
 sent a raw, scalding heat pouring through her.
He looked as though he was totally absorbed in her,
totally committed to her pleasure.

His hand touched her thigh, his fingertips stroking
lazily along the inside of it whilst she quivered helplessly beneath his erotic touch, gripped by seismic
shudders that pulsated through her body.

Soon he would find her wetness and when he did…
When he touched her there…

The erotic urgency of her own thoughts was only
adding to her torment. Xander was kissing the top of
her thigh, the inside of her thigh! His tongue was
pushing its way demandingly between the swollen
lips that should have been guarding her sex. She could
feel her own eager wetness. His fingers were parting
the lips of her sex, but it was his tongue and not his
fingers that discovered her ready eagerness for him,
tasting and savouring the intimacy of her as he ca-
ressed the engorged arousal of her clitoris.

It was impossible for her to sustain such an intensity of pleasure and even more impossible for her to
withstand it.

Her body arched and convulsed, and without thinking about what she was doing she reached urgently
for him, soliciting the hard, hot, silken thrust of him
within her.

Xander gave in to the need driving him and thrust
slowly and deeply into Katrina's waiting warmth.

Shudders of pleasure racked him as he felt her flesh
close firmly around him, her muscles holding him ca-
ressing him, as he was gripped by a savage, visceral
stab of white-hot reaction. He was supposed to be
doing this for her pleasure and not his own, to show

her…to give her something she would need so badly
that she would never, ever want any other man but
him. If he could not have her love, or her understand-
ing or her respect, then he would have her sexual
desire to hold her to him.

Only now the trap he had set for her had sprung
back on him and he was caught helplessly within the
moaning intensity of his need for her as he moved
fiercely within her, drawn deeper by the determined
female muscles, programmed to obey only Mother
Nature.

Katrina sobbed with fierce, elemental pleasure
against Xander's shoulder, shuddering intensely as
her body clung to every thrust of him within her, and
then contracted in a frenzy of convulsions that drew
from him not just his orgasm, but the seed of life
itself.

Releasing himself from her, Xander was bitterly
aware of what he had done. He got up from the bed,
leaving Katrina to battle against his rejection and her
own tears.

'I know he's your son, but I don't know how much
longer I can bear what he is doing to me.'

It was late in the afternoon and Katrina had come
as she so often did to the cool, shadowed downstairs
room that had been Xander's mother's library and private sitting room. Here in this room she felt able to
voice her most private thoughts and feelings, out loud
as though she were actually speaking them to a real
person. A person who was not just Xander's mother,
but also her own sympathetic and wise counsellor.
Someone who understood how she felt.

She had discovered the room when Miriam had

taken her on a tour of the villa, and somehow she found a solace here she could not find anywhere else, especially not the elegant bedroom where, every night in the privacy of its large bed, Xander took her in his arms and took her to both heaven and hell.

'I know he believes he is humiliating me, but the truth is that he is humiliating both of us! He hates me for my "Englishness", I know that, but I know too that he is your son and that he cherishes the memory of you, and you too were English. He speaks to me as though he believes I do not respect his cultural heritage, and will not listen to me when I try to tell him that he is wrong. I love the person he is—everything and all that he is, the unique blend of cultures and characteristics that have made him.'

Her voice dropped. 'I cannot stay with him. I love him so much—too much!—but my love for him is destroying me!'

On the other side of the swivelling bookcase, which separated the study that had been his mother's from the more formal office that had been his father's, which they had had connected by means of a secret swivelling panel, Xander stood stock-still. His heart was beating in long, slow, reverberating thuds that seemed to echo ominously in his own ears.

It shocked him to hear Katrina appealing so passionately to his dead mother. He could hear in her voice her loneliness and despair, and a pain he had never expected to feel entered his heart. He had heard what Katrina was saying quite clearly, but how could he believe it? It was true that she had vociferously told him what she thought of him and how much she hated him.

*　　*　　*

Anguish seized Katrina, locking her throat muscles and making it impossible for her to speak. Blinking away the threatening tears, she focused on the library shelves, remembering Xander's fury when she had accused him of stealing the books she now knew had been his mother's.

What if there were to be a child from this bitter-sweet intimacy they were sharing? Those long, dark hours of kisses and caresses, which she promised herself each time she would not allow to be repeated and yet every night she found she longed for again.

Had she no pride, no sense of self-preservation? Was she really so weak that she was ready to accept sex when what she ached for was love?

She heard the door open. It would be Miriam coming to see if she wanted anything! Quickly she snatched a book from the shelves and opened it, hoping to conceal her distress from the housekeeper.

'What are you reading?'

She stared in shock. It wasn't Miriam; it was Xander.

'I...er...' Apprehensively she started to retreat back into the protective shadows, but Xander followed her, plucking the book from her nervous grasp.

'These are the poems my father wrote for my mother.'

His words were almost an accusation, as though he believed that just by touching the small leather-bound book she had defiled it, Katrina recognised painfully.

'I know that the writing of poetry is part of Middle Eastern culture and that poets are honoured and respected for their work,' was all she could think of to say.

'*Their* poems are written for public consumption;

the verses my father wrote for my mother were not. They were his private avowal of his love for her.'

'You mean that I am not allowed to read them?' Katrina challenged him. 'Well, then, in that case they should not be on the library shelves!'

Suddenly she had had enough. Before she could weaken she burst out, 'This can't go on, Xander, and it isn't going to. I want to go home to England. I *am* going home to England,' she corrected herself. 'And nothing you can say or do will stop me!'

Before he could respond she fled, almost running past him and through the open door.

CHAPTER TWELVE

'YOU say you want to go back to England, but a marriage is not so easily put aside!'

They were in the bedroom, Xander having followed her upstairs.

'I don't care about that,' Katrina told him fiercely.

'No? Then what do you care about?'

He had walked past her, propping himself up on the door whilst he folded his arms and watched her.

Her heart was skittering around inside her chest in nervous anxiety. She cared about him. Him! And she cared far too much!

Deliberately turning away from him so that she wouldn't have to look at him, she said quietly, 'I don't like the way we are living. It isn't…right.'

'What do you mean?' Xander challenged her. 'What isn't right?'

He was baiting her, Katrina was sure of it.

Swinging round, she told him hotly, 'You know what I mean. During the day I hardly ever see you and when I do you virtually ignore me, but at night…'

She stopped, unable to go on.

'At night what?' Xander pressed her.

Katrina shook her head. 'You know what I mean.'

'At night I take you in my arms and your body responds so hotly to my touch that I scarcely—'

'Stop it!' The pressure of her own emotions was bringing her perilously close to breaking-point. 'I know how much you enjoy humiliating and tormenting me, Xander. You're a…sadist!'

'I can scarcely believe my good fortune in having as my wife a woman who gives herself to me so completely and who touches places within me I never imagined can be touched. No, I am not a sadist, Katrina. But I can't allow you to leave me.'

'Because you think there might be a child?' Katrina challenged him wildly. The words he had spoken had shocked her, but she refused to believe they were anything more than a calculated ploy to undermine her determination to leave.

'There isn't going to be a child, Xander!'

'No? You can be so sure?' he marvelled lightly. 'After all, it was only last night…'

'I knew this morning…' Katrina lied frantically, well aware that, whilst she might have spoken out loud when she'd been alone how much she loved Xander, she had not voiced her other secret—her growing suspicion that she might indeed have conceived Xander's child.

'Well, then, perhaps I had better make sure that there is to be a child,' Xander murmured. 'For I assure you that if there is, there is no way I will allow my child to go anywhere without me! Although you of course may not feel the same love and devotion to a child of our creating as I would…' His face hardened.

'Of course I would. I would love our child with all my heart,' Katrina answered him.

'So why then do you want to leave me?'

Katrina blinked and then stammered. 'I… I… We don't love one another, Xander.'

'You love me!'

She was probably gaping at him like a goldfish, Katrina decided dizzily as she went hot and then cold. How could he possibly know that? How did he know it to be able to state it so positively?

'I… What makes you think that?' she managed to ask him shakily.

There was a small pause, and then to her consternation he levered himself away from the door, and turned to lock it, placing the key in his pocket before he started to walk towards her.

'I heard you telling my mother.'

She had been sitting down on the bed, but now Katrina struggled to stand up, the better to confront her own nemesis.

'You couldn't have…' she whispered.

'But I did,' Xander assured her, slowly repeating for her her very own words, one by one as though he were tasting them first and finding them very much to his pleasure.

'I didn't mean it.'

To her disbelief he threw back his head and laughed. 'Liar,' he whispered back, but his whisper fell against her lips and his arms were already enfolding her and binding her to him.

The slow sweetness of his kiss was melting her mind and her inhibitions. It was impossible for her to resist him.

'You love me! Say it!' he demanded against her mouth.

'I do love you,' Katrina admitted woodenly as first one and then another tear spilled from her eyes and rolled down her face.

'Loving me makes you cry?' he questioned, catching the small drop of moisture with his fingertip.

'Love can hurt. My love for you caused me more pain than I thought I could bear.'

Katrina went completely still in his arms.

'Why are you saying that?' she demanded bitterly. 'You don't love me.'

'Of course I don't,' Xander agreed. 'And that of course is why I ignored everything I have always believed in to fight in the sand for you. Why I allowed El Khalid to force me into marrying you rather than lose you; why I took you to my bed even though I had promised myself I would not do so; why I hated myself with the deepest kind of loathing when I discovered that I had misjudged you and that you were a virgin. And that's why, too, it hurt me so badly when you refused to believe me when I told you those books had belonged to my mother; and why it hurt even more not to be able to tell you the truth about myself and who I was.'

'You never said anything,' Katrina told him in a small, agonised voice that betrayed her pain.

'Neither did you,' Xander pointed out gently. 'Marrying you a second time was a way of showing my strong feelings towards you.'

'I thought it was because the Ruler was insisting that you did. You said that it was…' she said, accusingly.

'After you had made it very clear that you found the idea of being married to me completely abhorrent!'

'I felt humiliated because I'd pleaded for you to be given mercy and then I discovered who you really were,' she said sadly. 'I imagined you laughing about it.'

'My sister-in-law told me that you loved me, but I refused to believe her.'

'I can't believe you love me,' Katrina murmured wonderingly.

'Would you like me to show you? I know you said you were... You said you knew today that you weren't pregnant...'

Katrina went pink.

'That wasn't exactly true... At the time I just wanted to get away from you.' She hesitated and bit her lip. Loving someone meant trusting them, didn't it?

'It is possible that I may be carrying our child, Xander, although it is far too soon to be properly sure at the moment,' she continued hurriedly.

Ignoring her, Xander reached out to cup her chin and tilt her face up so that he could gaze down into her eyes with a look of intensity and tenderness, and open and total commitment.

'There is only one thing I want more than for you to be the mother of my children, Katrina.'

'And what...what is that?' she asked him huskily.

'Your love,' he told her promptly.

'You have it, Xander.'

'And I shall cherish it and you for ever.' he promised her emotionally as he bent his head to hers and took sweet possession of her willing mouth.

EPILOGUE

'OH, XANDER, this is such a wonderful memorial to your mother and so very, very generous of your brother.'

'It is the perfect memorial to her,' Xander agreed as they stood side by side with other members of Xander's family whilst the Ruler officially opened the Women's University that had been built in Zuran in honour of Xander's mother and his governess.

'And it was you who suggested it.'

Katrina smiled lovingly at him as he hoisted their ten-month-old son a little higher in his arms.

'This isn't too much for you, is it?' he demanded anxiously, unable to stop himself looking betrayingly at the small bump of her new pregnancy.

'No, it isn't,' Katrina laughed.

'Pity,' Xander murmured wickedly. 'I was rather hoping we might have an early night tonight.'

HARLEQUIN®
Presents

Seduction and Passion Guaranteed!

Legally wed, but he's never said...
"I love you."

They're...

Wedlocked!

**The series
in which
marriages are
made in haste...
and love
comes later...**

**Look out for more Wedlocked! marriage stories
in Harlequin Presents throughout 2005.**

Coming in May:
THE DISOBEDIENT BRIDE
by Helen Bianchin
#2463

Coming in June:
THE MORETTI MARRIAGE
by Catherine Spencer
#2474

www.eHarlequin.com   HPWL3

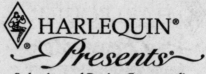

HARLEQUIN®
Presents~

Seduction and Passion Guaranteed!

**He's got her firmly in his sights
and she's got only one chance of
survival—surrender to his
blackmail...and him...in his bed!**

Bedded by... *Blackmail*
Forced to bed...then to wed?

A new miniseries
from Harlequin Presents...

Dare you read it?

Coming in May:
THE BLACKMAIL PREGNANCY
by *Melanie Milburne* #2468

If you enjoyed what you just read,
then we've got an offer you can't resist!

Take 2 bestselling love stories FREE!

Plus get a FREE surprise gift!

Clip this page and mail it to Harlequin Reader Service®

IN U.S.A.
3010 Walden Ave.
P.O. Box 1867
Buffalo, N.Y. 14240-1867

IN CANADA
P.O. Box 609
Fort Erie, Ontario
L2A 5X3

YES! Please send me 2 free Harlequin Presents® novels and my free surprise gift. After receiving them, if I don't wish to receive anymore, I can return the shipping statement marked cancel. If I don't cancel, I will receive 6 brand-new novels every month, before they're available in stores! In the U.S.A., bill me at the bargain price of $3.80 plus 25¢ shipping & handling per book and applicable sales tax, if any*. In Canada, bill me at the bargain price of $4.47 plus 25¢ shipping & handling per book and applicable taxes**. That's the complete price and a savings of at least 10% off the cover prices—what a great deal! I understand that accepting the 2 free books and gift places me under no obligation ever to buy any books. I can always return a shipment and cancel at any time. Even if I never buy another book from Harlequin, the 2 free books and gift are mine to keep forever.

106 HDN DZ7Y
306 HDN DZ7Z

Name	(PLEASE PRINT)	
Address	Apt.#	
City	State/Prov.	Zip/Postal Code

Not valid to current Harlequin Presents® subscribers.

Want to try two free books from another series?
Call 1-800-873-8635 or visit www.morefreebooks.com.

* Terms and prices subject to change without notice. Sales tax applicable in N.Y.
** Canadian residents will be charged applicable provincial taxes and GST.
All orders subject to approval. Offer limited to one per household.
® are registered trademarks owned and used by the trademark owner and or its licensee.

PRES04R   ©2004 Harlequin Enterprises Limited

eHARLEQUIN.com

The Ultimate Destination for Women's Fiction

Becoming an eHarlequin.com member is easy, fun and **FREE!** Join today to enjoy great benefits:

- **Super savings** on all our books, including members-only discounts and offers!

- Enjoy **exclusive online reads**—FREE!

- Info, tips and **expert advice** on writing your own romance novel.

- FREE romance **newsletters,** customized by you!

- Find out the latest on your **favorite authors.**

- Enter to win exciting **contests and promotions!**

- Chat with other members in our **community message boards!**

To become a member, visit www.eHarlequin.com today!

INTMEMB04R

HARLEQUIN®
Presents~

Seduction and Passion Guaranteed!

Introducing a brand-new trilogy by

Sharon Kendrick

THE
ROYAL HOUSE
OF
CACCIATORE

Passion, power & privilege – the dynasty continues
with these handsome princes...

Welcome to Mardivino—a beautiful and wealthy
Mediterranean island principality, with a prestigious
and glamorous royal family. There are three
Cacciatore princes—Nicolo, Guido and
the eldest, the heir, Gianferro.

Next month (May 05), meet Nico in
THE MEDITERRANEAN
PRINCE'S PASSION #2466

Coming in June: Guido's story, in
THE PRINCE'S LOVE-CHILD #2472

Coming soon: Gianferro's story in
THE FUTURE KING'S BRIDE

Only from Harlequin Presents

www.eHarlequin.com　　　　　　　　HPRHC

HARLEQUIN®
Presents

Seduction and Passion Guaranteed!

GREEK TYCOONS

They're the men who have everything—
except brides…

Wealth, power, charm—what else could a
heart-stoppingly handsome tycoon need?
In the GREEK TYCOONS miniseries you have
already been introduced to some gorgeous Greek
multimillionaires who are in need of wives.

**Now it's the turn of favorite Presents
author Lucy Monroe,
with her attention-grabbing romance**

THE GREEK'S INNOCENT VIRGIN
Coming in May
#2464

www.eHarlequin.com   HPTGIV